BEFORE PASSING

great
weather
for MEDIA

Printed in the United States of America

First Edition
ISBN: 978-0-9857317-6-2
Library of Congress Control Number: 2015910561

Editors: Jane Ormerod, Thomas Fucaloro, David Lawton, George Wallace, Russ Green
Guest Prose Editor: Chavisa Woods

Book design: Jane Ormerod
Cover photograph: Anthony Policano
Photograph of Bob Hart: Peter Darrell
Photograph of Anne Waldman: Nina Subin

Bob Hart's poem first appeared in *Tribes 12*
Anne Waldman's poem first appeared in *DukeCityFix*

great weather for MEDIA, LLC
New York, NY

www.greatweatherformedia.com

BEFORE PASSING

great weather for MEDIA

New York City

CONTENTS

INTRODUCTION

When the great weather for MEDIA editors began to asscmble this, our fourth anthology of poetry and short prose, we came to sense an imprint overlying the collection. The imprint left behind by our late friend Bob Hart. An elder in the New York poetry community for many years, Bob was not only an inspiration to and supporter of our work, he was looked on by all as the very personification of a performing poet. While his work was suffused with an understanding of Shakespeare, the Romantics and Poe, he was also captivated by the freshness of each novice poet reading at their first open mic. His focus remained on the process of creation itself, often giving away a new poem to a listener who admired it, or throwing an entire program away in the rubbish after its only performance. The sense of loss we felt was reminding us that it takes similar figures in other cities to build a writing community, and we cannot connect our communities without their inspiration.

This book collects writers from cities in twelve U.S. states as well as three foreign countries. great weather for MEDIA continues to tour in order to build on these connections, and this year brought our first readings in New Orleans and Cleveland, and first international events in Norwich and Manchester UK, as well as our annual west coast tour. Our writers were featured at PHILALALIA— Philadelphia's first annual small press and art fair, the New York City Poetry Festival, and the Rainbow Book Fair. We integrated music into our events, with John Sinclair in New Orleans and Venus de Mars here in New York. And we continue to welcome writers from all over to our weekly Spoken Word Sunday event at the Parkside Lounge. This past May, we published our third single poet collection, Corrina Bain's *Debridement*, to join our previous collections from Aimee Herman and Puma Perl. And in the next year, we will add collections from Wil Gibson and John J. Trause.

The title of our anthology, and the fragments of handwriting on the cover come from an unpublished poem of Bob Hart's, "Before Passing." It speaks to the passage of Time, and calls upon us to stop and take note of the world around us. Our featured poet in the anthology this year, the legendary Anne Waldman reminds us, in both her interview and sample poem, about the artist's obligation to question the decision making of our individual governments in terms of the well-being of our entire planet. And we are grateful to our guest editor Chavisa Woods for selecting prose pieces which (like the poetry that accompanies them) display their own sense of self-awareness through ideas of renewal and new beginnings, even within the very worst of circumstances.

So, before passing, take note of that time of year, when dead things gather and wait. Behold the dusk-tinged television antenna'd skies, the franchise chicken box with the starving god, the roadway littered with clown shoes. Heed The Herald when he speaks the forgotten names of the slain. See the cops do what they do. From open water to firm ground, the dry into the drink. Fly through the windshield and upon wings of wax. Directly to the bloodstream, practicing makeup tricks with a bunch of queens in the STD clinic. The liquor store in the train station. The other side of a goat trail. Hear that simultaneous wet and crunchy music of life. The river's endless coming and going. The sad black girls in all their ladyhood. That dude writing it all down fast on the Manhattan-bound A Train. A representative of the dead and the blind. Time strips everything from you but this moment. The working class joes in the automat give way to the trust fund kids in the cupcake café. Look for the charm of decay elsewhere. See what lurks within its depths. The impression people leave before they go, penetrating your atmosphere. On the pillow as they sink into sleep. *It is all, even the dark, light.*

That Time of the Year

NKOSI NKULULEKO

1.   It was that time of the year, again.
The leaves bronzed,
        became copper fields hitched to webs of branches.
Wind whistled through the blades of grass,
made their seasonal withering . . . tolerable in its company.
            The nights extended.   Day's breath . . . limited.
     A season to which all the dead things gather
                 and wait. and wait. and wait.

2. It is fall, my mother likes to dally up loose specs of dust dancing along the floors before the season hops off this dance floor. Mama's radio smolders the air with static, reminds her of her own being at times: a dismembered energy yearning to be deciphered. The day's singer: Whitney Houston. Mother cleanses the abode as a sung lyric foretells a woman's plight. How unseen she becomes as calendars shapeshift forward as she searches for a renewed self and who knew you could re-find the self in corners of dust? Only she, who knows wreckage to always be home for the most marvelous of things. The next day, we clean once again.--- Mother taught to make a home worth inhabiting. Years later, a friend of mine commits suicide, without even cleaning her room. I thought of that as a spiteful way of forbidding others to inhabit where she's already been. "Make a home worth inhabiting." I wish one could say that about the body, for such a ruined shrine it is. As if it were made out of debris, or rather some mannequin a god happened to insert breath into.---------------------

Day ends and moonlight pours through blinds, drenching our tiles in an icy blue, its glaciers draped beneath our feet, beguiling us to dance the chill of the night away in the fire we invoke. Shadows harbor the spectrums of us. A shedding of sorts. Remnants of We become dust. Skin, lantern-hue, peels at points, they scatter at the ends of this world, away from us as if it were contagious to dwindle in the nuance of the shining. And what a wonder it is, to know it is all, even the dark, light.

3. It is ahead of us, death.
   We, lightbulbs and lamp posts,
   Born to dim,
   Can only hope for our shreds of light,
   To drift down roads without us
   Like a legacy of some sort.

Define: What a Star Feels Like in My Mouth

DANIEL DISSINGER

this is where we start

on the lips
with a touch
of aspen leaves

turn and spin
and crunch

watch the edges click
together   and reach the tongue

her tongue
and throat

lit up
now

river water
caught

in this sound

like two hands find each other in some dark room

like breath in and out

like continuance

. . .

there is a house here
on the street
where you left me
and I am standing here
like so many torn white carnations
like a photograph singed at the folds
like complaints

yours is a language that seems hidden
inside his spine   and we want to taste that too

. . .

dear throat
I see you

all through the night

wandering in this city
the crevices of alleyways

look for someone's mouth

search the brick walls for more

language

she is
here

too

cover her face
and chest
and legs and face and arms
and chest and

tongue

where we meet

again

births a sound
perfectly ocean salt
and tension

this is the sexual
experience we are
all looking for

. . .

and he searches for him
searches for the blood

on each separated moment
throat lost now throat

you tempt him tempt us to(o)

walk alongside this edge

where pigeons grin
and complicate the landscape

may we find another place
to hide and capture that again

that rawness of scream and scream again

and rest draped in silk
for no reason

. . .

I enjoy you splayed
on the pillowcase

and revel in this
moment

we share . . .

The Herald

ELIEL LUCERO

There is a boom box blaring on this rush hour F train, held by what all think is just a crazy black man, who is hyping along the loud awful R&B, and none of us can pay focus on our distractions, so the lady across from me, not so politely asks the black man with the boom box to turn it down, and our ears hurt from the obnoxious highs of this tune, but the black man won't budge, and tries to negotiate a swap with his petitioner, but the white lady won't give up her seat in return for quiet, so we all try to ignore it, but these tweeters won't let us forget them, until the train is completely full, and everyone is holding on to each other, and the black man turns off his box, but not his voice, and he yells about Eric Garner, about the seven cigarettes in his pocket, how they would only amount to seven dollars, about the angry white cop who choked a man, unlike himself, to death for cigarettes, and some people are laughing, but I remember that the herald of the apocalypse would be madly insane, because he looked at the truth for too long, and he saw Anthony Baez murdered two decades ago by the larynx crushing forearm of a police officer, and he stood witness to Bell, and Diallo, and Grant, and Martin, and all forgotten names of the slain, and this herald knows to fear the serve and protect, but he is not afraid, he is yelling at the top of his lungs, he is asking for it, only so the truth could be known, that a black man must fear the blue, the arms, the suffocate, the taser, the fingers cocking pistol, the judge, the jury, so our herald is loud and brave, and can not shut up, or else we might not see it coming, and get swallowed alive.

Guy Bourdin's Girls Shed Their Lipstick

The decked-out ingénue with a touch of morbid fantasy . . .
—Anthony Haden-Guest, The New Yorker, 1994

DOROTHY CHAN

I. Eva Gschopf Writes to Bourdin

I loved how you put makeup on trees at night—
white maquillage on trunks, white nightgown for me,
all for a *Vogue* shoot—the makeup artist reddening my lips.
You were all about the rouge: red lips on pale skin—
red hair: you'd order mine pinned back,
controlling the waves—the waves you remembered of your mother.
You only saw her once in your life, and you made that known—
how you were merciless with women, thinking we looked better frail,
even dead. You'd mistake me for her, so if you controlled my hair,
you thought you finally controlled her.

But I wanted to be her. After all, she was your eternal muse,
the woman you ordered copies of: frail, gaunt ingénues
sporting flaming hair. I wanted rouge for life.
When I saw your photograph of a girl "spilling out"
red polish from her mouth, I wanted the real thing.
I wanted this real thing—the night I slashed my wrists,
hoping my fall into the almost-dead would garner your attention—
your art in my life. I was a martyr for your art.
I wanted this morbid fantasy with you—the first man
making me free as a bird, as I posed in a tree.

II. Wallis Franken on the Frankfurter

I was in a threesome before I was even sexually active.
Guy ordered hot dogs on top of mashed potatoes,
all on a silver plate, on set—and made me jump into bed,
with a doppelgänger of myself. I think she was a year younger.
"Feed her!" he barked. "Let those wieners choke her
until they reach her reflex! But close your eyes!
We can't lose the eyeshadow." He thought he was funny,
making jokes of our inexperience, making jokes of the "choking."
But I did find him funny. He made my doppelgänger cry,
which was perfect for me since she wasn't booked again.

Good riddance. I wanted to be Guy's only brown-haired-girl.
Sometimes all you want in life is an accomplice—
the more sinister and unyielding,
the higher your self-esteem.
Mine came in the form of a short, high-pitched
Frenchman-photographer. Guy would make hundreds of other
girls cry, and I'd laugh with him, also pushing them until
they cracked . . . until the day he sewed meat to my skirt,
wanting the dog to bite it. That crazy thing bit my leg.
The other model on set laughed. I ended up biting her leg.

III. Louise Despointes: Pearls Are Not a Girl's Best Friend

I remember holding the other girl after the shoot.
We looked like young lovers the way I embraced her naked flesh.
In reality, we both nearly died from glue covering our faces.
Guy was addicted to pearls. The makeup artist was covering
half our faces with glue, finishing it off with pearls,

21

until Guy demanded more pearls. "More pearls for fashion."
As I took the other girl's hand and we jumped into the bed,
I started losing focus . . . my eyes bleary . . . me starting to black out.
Eyes closed, I heard Guy's "Dead in bed? That's wonderful!"
when the artist later realized you need to leave a blotch of skin.

Years later, Guy would recreate the photo: black pearl edition.
Way to mock the situation. I wanted to punch the bastard.
I wanted to punch the makeup artist. I even wanted to punch
the other model for not realizing the dangers. I was tired of Guy,
tired of his endless "Well, you know you get paid" speech,
luring us to stay as his playthings, with money. He thought he
could just throw us around the room, throw us outside.
In reality, he did throw us around the room, throw us outside,
making me slave for a *Vogue* cover. Death was constantly dangling.

IV. Nicolle Meyer: Stopping Traffic

Guy made me wonder if all women are just actresses,
wanting to play the femme fatale, but actually acting the ingénue.
I was the unsophisticated girl, only 17 when I met him—
a dancer, unaware of his notoriety, until I was booked for a shoot,
and my head was missing or only my legs were showing.
It was all about legs and disco hair for Guy—
legs in colored tights, tied up on the train tracks:
girl sandwiched next to girl, when I wondered if all women
are in fact, not ingénues—but damsels, forever contemplating
who they want to end up on the train tracks with,

who they want to come to the rescue. But I was determined
to stop traffic instead . . . I was dressed in pastels,

instructed to lean over on the ledge as cars zoomed by.
Maybe I admired Guy for his gall—for his chew toy attitude
towards me. Maybe I wanted to be his damsel,
but in a daughterly way, so I could have an excuse to understand
the need to put women in danger.
It was all about the legs chopped off in pictures
At 17, I may have wanted a man to hold, caress my leg,
but what I craved was for the public to see my face—to see my face pleasure.

Woman with
a Blue Hat

KEN SAFFRAN

After Picasso,1925

no, it's a zebra celebrating
release from the boat firmly aground
now the world begins again
all green and new

Grief Is a Crouton

SARAH SARAI

Grief is a crouton that jumped from my salad
as it was to be chopped.
That's not really what grief is.
I just don't know.

One time I took an acting class.
I was asked, *What is your character feeling?*
I don't know, I said. *Yes, you do.*
So okay I had a clue, but not two sticks
I could rub together.

Pixelated memories, a scene out of tune,
regrets I've reconciled not once,
not twice, not thrice.
What comes after thrice?

Friends moldering in that great
affectation of eternity, an afterlife.
Aftereffects of pestilence, plague,
police action, stupidity, the plan.

Identification is forensic and learnable.
Doc, what you see on the corpse?
Petechial hemorrhage in the eyes,
and specks of grief beneath her nails.

When the in-debt leap into the Thames,
they stay sunk. It's lovers who learn
death is folly. Their fingers show signs of
clawing at stone and riverbank.
Everywhere, water, emotion's weight,
has sunk them. *Like a stone, you say?*
Ah, but at least they have known life
before being swept away.

An Urban Weapon

THADDEUS RUTKOWSKI

I brought a gun from my mother's house to my apartment in the city. The gun had been stored in her house since my father died. No one used it for hunting or target shooting anymore. It had been taken away briefly by my sister's husband, who looted the place after my father's passing. He'd piled some guns into a pickup truck and driven cross-country with them. My sister went along for the ride. She'd taken one of my father's paintings—it showed a silver zeppelin floating over a cornfield.

My sister's husband didn't have the guns for long. My mother took a plane to retrieve them. She just talked to the couple—she nagged them—until they gave the guns back. My mother had the guns shipped home. My sister and her husband kept the zeppelin painting. On one of my visits to my mother's house, I found the gun in its canvas case, propped in a corner of a closet. I unzipped the case and saw that the metal was blue, free of rust, and the stock was unscratched. The gun looked as good as new. I picked up the case by its leather handle and brought the gun home. I was in a car, so the cops didn't see me. No one stopped me.

*

I wondered if I needed a permit or license to keep the gun in the city. I looked up the laws. The city I lived in had the toughest restrictions in the nation. Handguns were clearly illegal, as were assault rifles and portable bombs.

My firearm couldn't be concealed—it was about five feet long. One of its barrels was threaded—that was the rifle barrel. Below the rifle barrel was a shotgun barrel, which wasn't threaded. This model was an "over-and-under," a sporting gun perfect for shooting wild turkeys. The rifle could drop a standing turkey a hundred yards away, while the shotgun could bring down a flushed turkey crashing through the trees above.

The gun didn't have a detachable magazine or a collapsible stock. It couldn't hold more than five rounds of ammunition—it could hold only two. It was not a semiautomatic weapon; you had to cock the hammer before firing. It couldn't be used to launch grenades. It was less illegal than a switchblade or a "throwing star"—the razor-edged disc Bruce Lee threw in movies.

I requested a gun registration form. I didn't want to break the law. But when the form arrived, I decided not to fill it out. Even though I had a right to own the gun, the registration fee was steep. I kept the firearm out of sight, propped in its case in a corner of a closet.

*

One night, my neighbor's place was robbed. He'd walked upstairs to talk to me, and he'd locked his door, but he hadn't shut the window leading to the fire escape. When he returned, he saw that the screen was torn and a stereo amplifier was missing.

He came back to my place to tell me what happened. I thought we should act fast. I owned a deadly weapon. If we saw someone with an amplifier under his arm, I would have the upper hand. I had the choice of firing the gun or just holding it in a threatening manner. "Drop the amp," I would say, "and step away. No one gets hurt."

But my neighbor thought that approach was overkill. "We don't need a gun," he said.

I picked up a hammer. I had never bludgeoned anyone, but I was ready to start. The invasion of our building had put me in high dudgeon.

My neighbor and I walked out to the street. There, we saw another neighbor. "I was worried," the other neighbor said, "when I saw a guy on the fire escape throwing something down to a guy on the street."

"What did it look like?" we asked.

"A stereo amplifier."

I hefted the hammer. It would do great damage if wielded like a club. "Where'd they go?" we asked.

"I have no clue," the other neighbor said. "They vanished into the crowd."

There were a number of pedestrians on the sidewalk and street. None of them were carrying an amplifier.

*

The son of a woman friend of mine stayed with me for an afternoon. He was eleven years old and I was his sitter. I thought the gun would amuse him, so I brought it out of its hiding place. I tried to explain how it worked. "It's an over-and-under," I said, "with a rifle on top and a shotgun on the bottom. If you see a turkey, you get one chance with the shotgun. Then, if the bird flies away and lands, you can try again with the rifle."

The boy picked up the gun and put it over his shoulder. He marched around the room, swinging his free arm and lifting his legs high. He looked like a soldier. He knew the drill. He would pass inspection.

"No, no," I said. "You cradle the gun in your arms as you hike through the woods."

I took the gun and cradled it, then walked around the room stealthily. I lived in a large, loftlike space, so I had plenty of ground to cover. "You kick the brush to scare up game," I said, as I made sideways motions with a foot.

When I came to the couch, my cat ran out of hiding. "There goes one," I said and raised the gun to my shoulder. The end of the barrel covered the animal. The cat didn't notice the danger—it had no experience with weapons.

I didn't pull the trigger. The gun wasn't loaded, anyway. The cat was safe.

"I don't want to hunt for animals," the boy said. "I want to be in the Army."

"You don't want to be in the Army," I said. "You might get killed."

"I want to see the movie *Dead Bang*, with Don Johnson."

When the boy's mother came to pick him up, she found out what we'd been doing. She got angry but tried not to show it. She just trembled and said, "I don't want my son in any home where there's a gun."

*

I went to visit my brother. One night, he brought out his collection of handguns. He had several semiautomatics. They were all loaded and ready to fire. He picked one up, removed the clip and worked the top action to make sure a cartridge wasn't in the chamber.

"Sight down the barrel," he said as he offered one of the guns to me.

I held the gun at arm's length and pointed it at a window. I lined up the bead with the rear notch. Any living thing in that pinpoint would be dead.

He picked another gun. "This one could start a war," he said.

He popped the clip out of the handle. "It holds fifteen rounds," he added. He showed me how the bullets were staggered in the wider magazine.

I didn't ask him if he had a permit or license to own the guns. I figured he could do what he wanted. He seemed to place great value on having the weapons. They were things that gave him a feeling of confidence, made him happy.

*

A friend of mine came to visit, and I told him about the gun I was keeping. "It's a hunting gun," I said.

"I'd like to take it out sometime," he said.

"You have nothing against guns?" I asked.

"I'm a Communist," he said. "I never know when I'll need to use a gun. The revolution could start anytime."

I brought out the gun, and we broke it down. We held up the barrels and looked through them from the back. We looked out through the front, the way bullets or pellets would travel. The shotgun barrel was smooth, and the rifle barrel had a clear spiral thread.

"Did you have to take a course to learn how to shoot?" my friend asked.

"Yes," I said. "The instructor set up a cabbage and told us, 'This has the consistency of a man's head.' Then he pointed a shotgun at it and pulled the trigger."

"My god," my friend said.

"Just showed what could happen," I said.

*

I remembered the last time I'd used the gun. I was a teenager, and I was hunting with my father. "Why don't you shoot?" he'd asked me. "What are you, gun-shy? The sound of a gun won't hurt you."

To prove his point, he fired his shotgun next to me. I tried to cover my ears, but I wasn't fast enough. The sound was the worst I'd ever heard.

Later, we were walking through some low pine trees, and I heard a grouse take off. I barely saw the bird—I only heard the drumming of its wings—but I lifted the heavy gun and swung the barrel along the bird's flight path. I "led" the invisible bird by a couple of feet and pulled the trigger. The blast was deafening.

I went to where I thought the bird might have fallen, but saw nothing but torn pine needles on the ground.

I stopped using the gun then. It was too heavy to carry and to shoot. I started to carry a lighter gun. After I moved out of my parents' house, I didn't hunt again.

*

I didn't know why I was keeping the gun. I wasn't going to hunt with it, and I wasn't going to use it to shoot at targets. I'd never shot a clay pigeon in my life. I wasn't a gun nut.

After storing the firearm for a while, I got rid of it. I took it back to my mother's house and left it there. I urged her to sell it—I didn't want her to give it to my sister and her husband. They weren't hunters; they were looters. They still had my father's zeppelin painting.

My Brother

FLOYD SALAS

He was bent in the shadow
of the same father
wore the same anvil of ignorance
like a hexer's charm
round his neck

But he glowed like a dark sun
while I was shrouded
black and white
and dusk grey
where the skin showed

Grey is the truer color
I wear it like a dark shroud
White is seen at dark
when only the lamp has eyes

But black catches the light more
like windshields in July heat
and hot tar on a wide street

All Your Trips to Saturn Have Been Tainted by Your Naïveté and Bad Luck

MEAGAN BROTHERS

you would like for a girl who
looks like winter
to kiss you in public,
outside the expensive hotel.
you would like to astound bystanders
with the tremendous volume of your love.
you would not like to hide with her
in apathetic gated gardens,
or scratch her name into your school desk
with a paper clip.
you would like to be a professional.
you would like to not fuck up the mission.
you would like to have plenty of money
and a name
so that when she calls it
it clicks right against her tongue,
it moves the rings and spheres,
it is the second half of hers,
it is tattooed on her corners,
it is the murmur of her dreams and
the watchword printed
on every piece of confetti

that falls from the sky
in your triumphant parade.
you would like to have a name
that declares in its saying
that you were victorious,
you won the princess and the prize.
you would like to have a name
that snaps like a snare
when she says it,
unlocking something vast,
so vast that you trip home
in lightspeed,
arranged in joy,
forgiving everyone.

the bottom of the bottle speaks (to queer youth):

LINETTE REEMAN

i know you. i've seen your

       lonely

          guzzle

   clicked the trigger
   of your finger

   rolled joint
   of your palm

           made barrel of

               your body
               my body

pulls the thin-blooded beg
from your lips so good
it's like we were *made*

   to down each

              other—
              kid,

did you think
you'd grow up

                                        weapon?

all this ache

shotgun-cocked against
flat palm batcave-beat
against hairy thigh against

        the liquor store   in the train station

                where this town

                                dumped

                your soggy

                                        melody—
                                        kid,

        did you think
        you'd grow up

                                        spectacle?

        when they helped

circus your suicide
note, told you "come back
normal, or come back
dead"—did you think

you would?

cause whatever

you are, you're not

normal. that's why

the smoke makes

home

of your lungs, why

your parched makes

dance

of my innards
that's why you

break

so

easy

The First Time
I Bit Someone
Since I Was Two

ALEPH ALTMAN-MILLS

I was all fistbone, the only part of me
the liquid red voices couldn't curl around.
My brain had been
unsharpened in the rock polisher
but my teeth were a mouse trap;
they knew their job.

To Sad Black Girls

KEAH BROWN

You are a greenhouse. Let light catch your hidden petals.
You are the moon that chases the streetlights, dance with them for a while.

They will try to change you. You will feel small.
They will tell you that your features are only beautiful on someone else's skin
—but we know that's not true.
Your lips, your eyes, your hips and thighs are silk dipped in honey.

To sad black girls:
Who press knives into their skin.

Who break their bones the way
They break bread,
Trying to fit in.

To sad black girls:
Who cry themselves to sleep at night.
Know that you are an ocean that doesn't stop for a lake.
Don't bite your tongue so they can taste your blood.

To sad black girls,
They don't know you like I do. I know you're tired and angry.
They break your heart into a million little pieces every single day.
You dig your nails into the palms of your hands because
You want to feel something other than empty. I feel it too.

But you are beautiful, you are enough.
You are enough.
You are enough.

To sad black girls:
I'll speak your name. I'll tell the world that you feel too.
I'll make sure that if no one says so today, tomorrow or next week, I love you.

Cartology

KAREN HILDEBRAND

I was conceived in the house of 2211 (Center Street)
These are power numbers
An auspicious sign, multiplied—two two one one
the world proceeding in pairs
I flipped my luck and lived at one one two two (Gaylord)
with a gay lord, no less
When is 2 a binary number and when is it a duel?
We added up the columns and split.

Double or single? This is always the question
for those born under a Gemini moon
Lesson #2119 (South Sherman)
I took back my family name and lived
under the sign of restless
3895 Rings of Saturn
2222 House of Chaos
Venus rising
room of sorrow
jellyfish cocoon.

My sun is in the number 6—
the great explorer
6 digit salary
sex, serpentine

fetal, the frame
for all smart quotations
106 (Pineview)
616 (Carolina)
61 (West 10th)
Where is my six now?

I'm back to simple math.
Two aught one (Clinton)
solve for double vision
minus the repetition
wobbly, bobbly, no love for me
If it's all a numbers game
dear wheel of fortune
why not throw me a lucky 7?
All sharp edges, slanty sideways glances
a crushed velvet fainting couch.

Mutants Make No Apologies

GINA WILLIAMS

A hadrosaur mummy, having endured a polar winter, holds its frozen gaze while she coats her lips, stroking, side to side, bottom to top, greasing the contours of chemically entranced cells with the grease of the damned. "Whore paint," the righteous uncle called it one Christmas while puffing on a cigar, hand-rolled by little girls, somewhere, down there. Reptile skin contains billion-year-old compounds, the building blocks of life, the same ones that leapt from the lizard brain of the idiot boy just yesterday. The one who called the girl a damned bitch, before coffee, before the chance to mate, which must have been a shame, but you get what you get. The reptile epidermis, that delicate light-reflecting stratum as precious as feathers rests in the shade until the painted lady saunters by, whereupon the dewlap swells in a sweetly disturbing display, all silenced musk and bugle. Reality television blurs the deliciously mundane commonalities of life on earth but science is our destiny, lashing us not lightly with salted rope until the last fossil, the final clinging molecule, is at last leached by fire and erased by wind and we are turned loose, shuffling clawed feet, sniffing at the moon and hanging our scaly heads as we crawl, single file, into the solar night.

pH

TATYANA MURADOV

I drink you because I need you to turn me into something good;
tea and honey are one thing, but whiskey,
well damn baby
that's all you
I've got ulcers to prove it
you're no milk and cookies
you burn through me
acid rain
coca cola
sour patch
you eat at me
I am 95 lbs of natural erosion
no diets necessary, just a whole lotta love to give and nowhere for me to put it.

LadyHood

LATEESHA BYNUM HINTON

For the ones that like to be entered often
And the ones that are sometimes soothed
Congrats on being a lady
For the ones that scream at the top of her lungs
And let the truth be known
Congrats on being a lady
For the sisters that roll their eyes and necks
Congrats
Riding with the public on the public
Carrying bags and burdens
Dealing with him, her, and them
You are doin' it with style, your style
Congrats on being a lady
Hair from the store on the corner
Jewelry and lashes and shoes from the same
Hair from the Mother Land
Hair on the floor
When we see you
Yes, You
We see a Lady
Some teeth gold, some not
And
You are still a lady
Most men gone, a couple not
And you
Yes, you
Are still a lady

Particle Fever

STEVE DALACHINSKY

1. we rely too much on the luck of others:
    he talks to himself – a dry-brained mouthy word machine
    rubs the silver residue from the numbers   to see if he has won
    $50 that's not even enough for a happy birthday
    that's it – a happy birthday   805   3 whatever it is – it's a constant *mumble*
    # 1 most   3 again too low 8 for me to here 1st avenue
    5 *(inarticulate)* i could still take the 3rd avenue bus
    it's a living right / *very old foreign accents*
    he's so busy seeking his fortune that he totally misses his stop
    long line – you can get off here take a number 1 to a number 6 or an
    A or E or C or F at west 4th – these aren't numbers but they work
    fortunes made & lost – particles smashed together & separated
    circling each other like dueling swordsmen or lovers or flocks of lost birds
    more long lines > dual identities
    we are given a perfect blend of city & country   stone blood concrete & space
    where it all began – the essential world both real & imagined
    a blank slate –   invoked ersatz & computer imaging
    the picture we see > the result of this bombardment is just a re-enactment
          happening precisely while the real thing is or isn't / happening
    a sign on a store on a once smelly fish stained Chinatown street
        says **WARM** - says – **HIPPIES WELCOME** –
                says   *look for the charm of decay elsewhere*

    now he only talks to birds & counts the spoons
    breaks twigs in his mind & waits for his number to hit.

2. he dreams of a new physics – his memory muscle remembering little
    he awakens under pressure – dismisses the event as a disaster
    a new EDEN that can never be – just more media hype
    the long line – an eruption of interruptions – an endless ellipsis
    a song eclipsed – reading the melody upside down / backward
    & we are left with a short line that sounds too much like the original
    say #6 – the last in the order even tho there are 7 parts
    7 tho the original had only 3 – but he keeps scratching
    for how long will this go on – scratching   mumbling short sentences
    long lines – all waiting for the media to watch as the wonders begin
    an omniverse – a multiverse within supersymmetry –
        an elucidated secretly overweight universe –
    overweight women discussing their dating habits over hamburgers
      the long line enters again – wish / risk / a backlist of sales reps
    fabiola nobodies adept at tomfoolery / expanding warehouse precedentals
    new equipment   backward promotions   & lovers of the death machine
        at a loss for words: the thing is *the things which* >
            art & science colliding   the science of art the art of science
                        do the math it's all there scratch head 7 / 5 13 / 22 / uh
    long only as the wind dreams / *are least important to our survival* / THE UNIVERSE
    reverse rhythms / the long line / eclipsis / *are the things that make us human* /
      a place to inhabit / visit / able as we are NOT / 400 years of symmetry /
      400 years of slavery / the Blakean theory of the universe / multiverse /
                FEARFUL SUPERSYMMETRY
    beams   auto-clavé   proposal ATLAS   high COLLSIONS energy

                DREAM: poetry & the possibility of sensual sex
            dream of physics / taking physics / rumble of the bus tires
        idling of the engine / vibration of the shocks / motionless stoplight / bumpy ride
          circling & circling & circling / finally colliding / pudding just for you /
    high priest of the good ear / ta(i)nn(t)ed / complimentary speak lady / mute-on
      electron/ neutron / to hold her beholden / he scratches & scratches rubbing off the

numbers / then the collision / not 115 for supersymmetry / not 140 for a multiverse but
somewhere in between a 126.5 or 125.6 / so there might be a continuation of something
somewhere / or a falling apart   & i say the fix is in
a few more years of experimentation that tell us where the beginning ends & the ending
begins   & the GOD PARTICLE still somewhat elusive / adida amira right there
   a warm february night / it's right there / the assimilation of different styles / the
absorption of different solar systems / the realization that he's won very little /
his head suddenly slumping into his knees / nothing / 1 / 3 / birthdays / 8 / 1st avenue / 3rd
avenue / 6th avenue / missed chances missed stops / the wrong bus /
lexington avenue / the hickscups / the goddamned GOD particle / that keeps our lives
together / that tears our lives apart / a disabled wheelchair / a brief pause /
this ersatz motionless priority of property / you must give up i tell him / he looks /
    scratches   /// \\\\ *whatever* – he replies – it's the red hand of GOSH – i almost
scream – *whatever* – it's right there – i point nowhere – *whatever* – he looks / scratches /
GIVE UP – I loudly whimper – he gets up – whatever he mumbly whimpers – IT'S
RIGHT THERE – he bumbles he scratches – *so far so good* he ciphers
all that grey matter grey stuff grey particles grey dust grey ghosts all those numbers
collisions where they all go? wrong stop – you'll have to walk a bit
                have a good one i say – i'm getting off here –
                  the cross fire of an avalanche
                  a cavalcade of transitional #s
though his atoms have been split time & time again he still cannot find
                  the center of his being
        where is form when we need it \ or at least a semblance of form
            i exit first   the long line   wait i say   or don't wait
there's 1 to 6 or A or E or C or B or F or D   & all this equals 21 –
          what color is tonight? the GOD particle asks me
            turn the paper upside down's my answer.

Accidental Lover

ALEXIS RHONE FANCHER

This is no accident.

Feelings are involved, dammit.
Bodily injury. Emotional distress.

In the oncoming rhapsody of her headlights, you
see your sixth birthday, the bumper cars.

When you connect, your tape-looped
head smashes against the windshield.

Don't be surprised when the paramedics
pull the sheet over your face.

Your sweet mama's ghost
will shine a light.

Aim for the high beams,
the blindside;

focus on her final release.

Revel in the impact,
the ephemera of Truth,
the hard fast pleasure in
shifting
down.

INTERVIEW

The Cosmos Came to Me
and Said
It Didn't Like Fracking

Aimee Herman: In the anthology *Civil Disobediences: Poetics and Politics in Action*, which you co-edited with Lisa Birman, you wrote, "There is currently—and one feels this is not going to go away—a strange and disturbing disjunct or rip in our culture that calls for an articulate active repressive agenda where anyone who doesn't agree with current USA administration junta policies is unpatriotic." This book arrived in 2004. Eleven years later and these slashes against our culture are getting louder. What are your thoughts on current civil disobediences? Furthermore, in what ways can poetry stand up and activate change?

Anne Waldman: Poetry can move the psyche forward, can help wake the world up to itself. That was something Allen Ginsberg and I expressed and considered in the mission of the Jack Kerouac School at Naropa University. It's a very subtle process individually, personally. Your own work captures and mirrors your own psycho-physical rhythms, genetic streams, your animal spirit and passion. Even if you are a "conceptual" writer you are reflecting back some "news." I write to understand my own consciousness, my sense perceptions, the relationship between "I" and "Other." I write to celebrate my world and the multiverse and to play inside language which has no bounds. Imagination which has no bounds. I imagine an alternative reality. All the work—to borrow Frank O'Hara's apt title—are "Meditations in an Emergency." Frank continues to wake the world to itself. There's no formula for the right activist poetry. I am working on a few pieces currently: *Melpomene* which investigates transmutation of tragedy, and *Future Feminism* which is a romp of the old tropes. Also a meditation on William Blake's "Book of Thel." These projects seem relevant to my own survival. And the "Jaguar Harmonics" poem and musical suite are a larger look at the cosmos through the eyes of the entheogen, Yage. The cosmos came to me and said it didn't like fracking.

But indeed, the slashes go deeper. The violence is very palpable, and there's a collective need, as artists, as cultural workers, to continue the struggle toward a greater version of peace and justice, race and gender equality, and accountability of those hired and trained to protect the civil state. In our own country and wherever else we can be of service. And the climate issues are urgent and not going away. The radical climate change isn't waiting for us to get our act together. We have all experienced some of the recent calamities of floods and fires. Our Summer Writing Program cottage is condemned because of black mold after the floods in Boulder. We've had programs interrupted by the toxic smoke from fires.

So many artists lost valuable and irreplaceable work during Hurricane Sandy. Our streets of late are battlegrounds. But I was impressed with the perspicacity of a recent lie-down event in Washington Square Park, New York City, protesting the Mike Brown and Eric Garner murders (before the bigger march a week later, also amazing). The UN definition of genocide was read aloud and repeated. There is a case here, a legal case, for the accusation of genocide against the United States.

I recommend that people "tithe" their time, pick their battles, join networks that specifically inspire you to action, stay connected, and put voices and bodies (when possible) on the line. Civil disobedience is important but you want to be wary of agent provocateurs. You want to have a skillful plan. You want to join with an ethos you can support. When the camera turns to you, you want to be able to speak with knowledge and vision. You want to read a poem that has reverence and conviction. There are poems for such occasions. How can you be most effective, articulate, participatory? You might want to work behind the scenes in support roles. What are your skills in addition to being a poet, an artist? and so on. And voting is important in spite of my anarchist leanings. Certain changes will only happen through vote, courts of law and so on. We can't be naïve. The next election is a time to go public with more humanitarian agendas. As a Buddhist I want to advocate anything that eases suffering.

Aimee Herman: You have created, and been involved in, socially conscious spaces for decades. How does political impact play a part in what you write? So many poets and writers have been banned and/or reprimanded because of their language. Amiri Baraka and Allen Ginsberg immediately come to mind. Baraka's poet laureate status was threatened by New Jersey Governor (at the time) McGreevey due to the controversy over his poem, "Somebody Blew up America." Ginsberg's "Howl" caused a famous censorship court case in 1957. In *Civil Disobediences* you wrote, "No one wants to be 'dissed' on this planet, more people and life forms need to be heard from." Do you ever worry about censorship? How does this affect or influence your poetic practice?

Anne Waldman: Censorship is not quite the same issue in 2015. My work is not as confrontational as Amiri's. I was able to travel around the world with a piece, *Neuro-linguistically: This is the Writing Dance*, in which I symbolically strangle Donald Rumsfeld and Dick Cheney. And I performed "Rogue State" on Wall Street. I throw out spells and curses. The NSA knows I am at heart a Buddhist. The work is more shamanic than terrorist. I am not on their radar these days, I think. But I worry about the survival of The Poetry Project into the distant future, about the survival of Naropa University and its priceless archives. These communities are at risk. These larger constructs that harbor genius and vision so threatened in a super capitalist agenda, depend on erratic funding. They don't have huge endowments, and are not institutionalized in those normal ways. And many smaller venues that need space and support go under. What a vapid world without the alternative cultures.

Aimee Herman: Anne, the first time I saw you perform was in Boulder, Colorado. I felt like I was watching you give birth to new words and sounds. How do the incantations arrive for you? Watching your body sway, it is as though you are dancing with the echoes of each word. You've collaborated with musicians including your son Ambrose Bye. How does music play a part in your writing process?

Anne Waldman: Music is inherent in the language. Melopoeia is always present—it is the undertow. Ambrose grew up with my sounds and rhythms and he accompanies and creates sound structures for the texts beautifully. Often sounds-in-making, as I call them, come before words. The musical plan for "Jaguar Harmonics"—an hour-long "suite" for want of a better term—is basically improvisational within certain parameters. The piece includes cello, saxophone, trumpet, keyboard, various percussion instruments, with Ambrose's tinkerings and my text and vocals. It is measured and wild at the same time.

Aimee Herman: Are there any poets, writers, artists who you would like to collaborate with but haven't yet?

Anne Waldman: Antony! Bhanu Kapil! I've been enjoying the open structure of Fast Speaking Music which includes family (Ambrose, plus my nephew Devin Brahja Waldman on sax) and others who come into the mix: Thurston Moore, jazz genius Daniel Carter, the cellist Ha-Yang Kim. Max Davies in Boulder. I did a brief recording with Meredith Monk and I'd love to do more with her. The musicians of ARoarA based in Montreal are brilliant and we are working on an album based on my book, *The Iovis Trilogy: Colors in the Mechanism of Concealment*. Andrew Whitman is overseeing that project. Ha-Yang and I have the "Hungry Ghost" sonata. I want to do more with Jesse Paris Smith, playing her harmonium. I want to continue to work with Eleni Sikelianos in vocal performance. So already there's a lot being generated. I also work with my husband, filmmaker Ed Bowes, helping with some of the writing and production. The new project is entitled *Gold Hill*. I'd love to do another collaboration with Eileen Myles. And Thomas Sayers Ellis would be a terrific poet to work with—I like what he does in performance. The dancer Yoshiko Chuma and I are thinking of something. Art projects with Pat Steir, Donna Dennis, and Pamela Lawston continue. It goes on and on. I love working with others. My idea of the sacra conversazione . . .

Aimee Herman: Do you feel like you are still gathering new practices in your writing? It seems unfair to ask you *how do you write?* (Perhaps it is easy enough to answer: with pen and paper. Or through an open mind.) But would you mind sharing some of your methods? Particular places you find comfort when writing? Are there certain songs or sounds you like to play?

Anne Waldman: A lot of spontaneity, open mind, etcetera, but I am doing research on the Buddhist sense of the unborn, angelology, and rainbows for my Blake project. Some hint—some luminous detail—will often come in a dream. I got an interesting letter at Naropa asking if I could locate a person recommended by me to this person in a dream he had of me. That set up some interesting meanderings. I worked on a libretto for an opera commission, *Artaud in the Black Lodge*, referencing Antonin Artaud, William Burroughs, and David Lynch. I liked comparing the three in my research and setting up a mandala of the Six Realms to place some of the material into.

Aimee Herman: In 1974, you co-founded the Jack Kerouac School of Disembodied Poetics at what is now Naropa University in Boulder with Allen Ginsberg and Chogyam Trungpa Rinpoche. I remember taking a creative writing class at a community college in Hartford, CT many years ago. My teacher said, *Aimee, you must apply to this school. You can make noise with your words there.* He was right. Naropa is a unique learning environment; it embraces activism, spirituality and freedom regarding language and writing. What was your intent when starting this school and how do you feel higher education guides creative writers? What are your thoughts on the influx of poets with MFAs?

Anne Waldman: I think Naropa offers a unique experience for a creative writer, and the Summer Writing Program creates a community you might not find elsewhere, whether you are a degree student or not. All kinds of writers arrive. Many from outside the more official verse culture mainstream. And we have an extraordinary archive that students and scholars can draw on, started from the beginning of the school in 1974. The intention was to "not take criticism from someone who had not produced a notable piece of work" (Ezra Pound adage) and to *read* poetry as well as write it. Not so much emphasis on "workshopping." (That dreadful term.) And have the backdrop of a meditative environment. My take is that there's a glutted market in the MFA grad flux. The jobs teaching are finite. We encourage our students to think outside that usual career box—become a printer, an infrastructure activist, an editor, a translator, a performer, a hobo, a cine-poem artist, etcetera.

Aimee Herman: When you travel, what books do you take with you? Poetry, prose, non-fiction? What are some recent collections that have made their way to your bookshelves? Are there any writers you rush out to read?

Anne Waldman: All categories always. I carried the Karl Ove Knausgaard trilogy on a trip to France. Laird Hunt, Claudia Rankine, Giorgio Agamben, Ammiel Alcalay, Alice Notley, Will Alexander, Jackson Mac Low, Arthur Sze, Eimear McBride, Andrea Rexilius, Joe Ceravolo, Eileen Myles, Mei-mei Berssenbrugge, the new Baraka reader coming up, North African poetry . . . the list goes on.

Aimee Herman: You are extremely supportive toward archival projects and have helped document various readings and texts which might otherwise have been lost. We are living in a society where everything is documented. What do you think is worth preserving?

Anne Waldman: The annals of The Poetry Project, the annals of the Jack Kerouac School. These countless hours of lectures, panels, colloquia, workshops, readings, and performances are worth preserving because they let people of the future—grappling with the endless human struggle—know that some of us were not just slaughtering one another. You might want to read my allegorical book-length poem, *Gossamurmur*, which is an allegory about the rescue of poetry's oral archive.

Aimee Herman: Anne, in your poem "Steps of a Bodhisattva" (from *Structure of The World Compared to a Bubble*) you wrote, "In this stage the adept is you / Adapting to the place you are, the spot you are / Adapting to the structure of your own commerce / Start here." You have traveled extensively and I wonder if there are spots that have become soul nourishments? Can you share a moment where, upon adapting, you started to see the structure of yourself become clearer?

Anne Waldman: In the Ellora Caves in India, near Aurangabad, I felt part of a continuum that was in a full joyous transmigratory flow. The sculpted stone in various panels is very cinematic. It moves, it vibrates, the deities become alive. I saw myself as Chamuda, the old hag. I saw myself as bird, as tree, as monarch, as warrior, as dancing girl, as not so alien to this place and complicated continent far from home. The structure sometimes wobbles, but I think you can travel anywhere with your attuned consciousness. And to places—often—that most need you.

Author of over forty books, ANNE WALDMAN is a poet, writer, editor, performer, teacher, cultural/political activist, and a creator of radical hybrid forms for the long poem. She is the author of the magnum opus *The Iovis Trilogy: Colors in the Mechanism of Concealment* (Coffee House Press, 2011); a feminist "intervention" taking on war and patriarchy with a Buddhist edge, which won the PEN Center 2012 Award for Poetry. Her book *Gossamurmur* (Penguin, 2013) is an allegorical adventure and plea for poetry's archive which "reanimates sentient beings." *Jaguar Harmonics*, her newest collection, was published by Post-Apollo Press in 2014. A prolific editor, Waldman's latest anthology, co-edited with Laura Wright, is *Cross Worlds: Transcultural Poetics* (Coffee House Press, 2014). Waldman helped found and direct The Poetry Project at St Mark's in the 1960-70s and went on to co-found The Jack Kerouac School of Disembodied Poetics at Naropa University with Allen Ginsberg, where she continues to curate the Summer Writing Program. Widely travelled and translated, Waldman has worked most recently in Morocco, India, and France. She is a recipient of the Shelley Memorial Award and a Guggenheim Fellowship for 2013-14.

Drop of Shiva's Semen Shot into the Ocean Now Swallowed by a Fish

ANNE WALDMAN

Drop in the ocean, all world one
becoming monstrous: what happens Mumbai happens Bombay
what happens Vicenza U.S. Base or Prodi, Kyoto Accord, XL Pipeline
advanced warplanes to Japan - what happens? Egypt, Yemen, Syria
NASA's five space probes or Aurora Borealis where we study shimmering light
what happens on Lunar New Year
I want to know are there names for these moves and mores?
a lexicon and vibration that touches the complexity of gestural motion
what happened with Augustine & his mother in Ostia?
I want to know what happens Nicea 325
perhaps God creates the world! *Ex nihilo Ardore/splendore*
Europe still riding the pull of Zeus a nuclear reactor not dismantled
& how that is part of your story - flooding in Mozambique, a part of you
what happens Rwanda, Darfur, Chad, glaciers shrinking what happens
carbons capped bombs falling on Natanz? what is the poet's job out of slumber?
entering post-modernity I gave my soul away - started chanting Om Ah Hum
for the Year of the Gun Metal Rabbit
and the Year of the Shimmering Golden-locked Ram

From the Horde

for Nina

RACHEL THERRES

she is a boot-smashed Tuesday
barbed tongue, two fists full of stripped wires
flickering, smoke curling from their dragon necks

she is the bombshell peeled
back to explosive dust
black scattered confetti ground into pavement cavities

she is the bomb shelter
protection without riveted walls
cherry pits gathered in small armies

she is an undone skin of dress
a tangle of ruffle and zipper entrails
a wick's end sighing into an apology of smoke.

Phantom Poem Syndrome

for Joel Landmine

RICH FERGUSON

it's the unspoken words
lying fallow on the tongue.

it's the ghostly limb
sprouting from the heart;
shadow & vacuity
its flesh & bone.

it's the things you can't quite reach—
the off switch on your fear machine,
or the gratitude grenade
to obliterate discontent.

it's everything in your brain,
restless & raging;
a chainsaw with ADD.

it's the suicidal tendencies
moving at terminal velocity.

it's the gun
that can't stop jonesing
for a wild & hating hand
to keep its barrel warm at night.

Everything Changed after 9/11

AMBER ATIYA

christmas eve sister hands me a zip-locked bag
stuffed with travel-size shampoo, tooth brush, lavender-scented
lotion, medallion of white soap.

got this from the people givin goodies to the homeless.

what people?

i dunno, just people.

thirty-three degrees, her ankle length coat
has no lining.

ain't nothin lined anymore. no one who don't live
on park avenue is entitled to lining.
or hot water. or fresh pears.

me, the bamboo, the basil plant, the aloe leaf
the e and j on the kitchen table, all listening,
taking notes.

she has come to use the internet, to print a pass
to shower at the Y.

they take mugshots.
you cannot shower at the same Y twice.

she has showered at every Y in queens.
she has showered at half the Ys in brooklyn.
one in the bronx.

no one knows you on staten island
i say.

no one knows me
on staten island. her voice, cheerless.

they still allow shoppin carts on the ferry?
everything changed after 9/11.

once, transit cops in penn station forced a woman to remove
her prosthesis. they jabbed her with batons.

she screamed for help. hopped in circles
in a yellow sock.

what the cops do then
i ask.

she sucks teeth, grabs glass, pulls cork
out the brandy.

they did what they do.
laughed.

yup.

and then cuffed her.

Early Morning

THOMAS HENRY

If you must know,
my address is the woods,
where I grow fat on rabbits,
chipmunk meat, and squirrels
with all the fruits, nuts,
herbs and spices
I could ever need.
There's sassafras here,
goat weed, crab apples
and did you know
that prickly ash grows spicy little berries
with Szechuan peppercorns inside?

There's a sun and a moon
that I share with every one
but the air here is mine,
all mine.

It seems like our collective memory
has forgotten about space, solitude,
the rising and setting of the sun,
a day's work bringing about necessary things,
death, decay, and silence.

Silence isn't a complete absence of sound
just the sounds people make.
In the deepest silence,
there is still the rhythmic voice
of wind and rustling,
birds and insects,
water,
the howling of wolves,
the crackle of a flame.
That simultaneously wet
and crunchy music of life
that can only be heard in silence.

Do I ever miss city life
with its conveniences and
cultural trappings of human existence?
Do I ever want to return?

Maybe,
but only for a visit.
I'm all set out here in the woods
with no visitors and no excitement,
only books, squirrels, trees, fire, and
pages and pages of writing.

Kangaroo

VICTORIA HATTERSLEY

Was it eating her insides raw, like a parasite? And if so, did that mean she was the host? Or hostess, to be more accurate. She'd never been a particularly good hostess. It wasn't that she objected to other people exactly. She just lacked the gift for wholehearted welcome.

Of course, there was nothing she could do to help herself now. Even if it was. Eating her. Feeling a slight disturbance from her swollen mid-section, she drew up her shirt and looked down. In time to see something small and foot-sized press itself up against the hardened wall of her stomach.

There was an old lady who swallowed a fly, she thought. And laughed, softly.

All this crap people had told her about the beauty of pregnancy. Womanly curves. Blooming. Secretly she'd always found it revolting. Obscene and unnatural, she thought. Like a question mark turned upside down so it's thrown back on itself. Smug and unknowable to anything but itself.

And children knew too much, so she didn't trust them. All the more curious then that she was incubating one. And she was unsure how it had happened. Of course she knew how it got there. She wasn't the vessel for the Second Coming. But the part in between was blurred.

She sat alone by the edge of the still lake. Among the insects and the long grass.

*

The man, or boy, with the guitar had been getting progressively drunker. He might have been even older than her, but he swigged from his can like a fifteen-year-old let loose at their first house party. What interested her was that the drunker he got, and the more he slurred, the better he played. By about 11:17 p.m. he'd turned into a vague approximation of Carlos Santana. Except he couldn't sing by this point, so she did it for him.

She had no idea where he came from or which of her friends, if any, he knew. But she didn't ask, because it didn't matter. When he couldn't play anymore, he said "You sound angry when you sing. Like Janis Joplin."

"Was she angry? Have you met her?"

"I don't know. Is she dead?" His face screwed up for a moment. Like a toddler using words it hasn't yet given meanings to.

"Of course. Very."

He giggled, showing yellowish teeth. "I'm very drunk." Then he stopped and for a moment she was afraid he might cry.

"Where are you from?"

"I'm Scottish."

"You don't sound it." He sounded like Toad of Toad Hall.

"I am. Where I'm from the sheep have Velcro legs."

"Are you visiting someone?"

"I don't know."

Later on he jumped naked into the black lake. ("I don't think it's natural to wear clothes when you're swimming.") He returned shaking water out of his hair like a dog. She handed him a dubious blanket she'd found. They lay on the grass and looked for bats. Some people were still drinking, although most had gone home. The fire was dying. Poking it coaxed it into brief death-spasms of cascading sparks.

When the fire had given up entirely, they retrieved his guitar, his rucksack, and a half-empty bottle of whiskey someone had left behind. They made their way to her house. Several months later, he was still there.

*

The first ultrasound. Lying back in the dark room, looking down at her flat midriff, she'd found it implausible that there was room in there for something to exist. The smiling female smoothed a viscous alien-spew over her. And then began pointing at things on the screen to the right of her.

"Look. There are its arms and legs. Too soon to tell the sex now obviously, but it's certainly a mover."

Gestation. That was what her body was doing. A herd of pregnant elephants trampled briefly over her brain.

The creature on the screen was indeed waving its spindly ultrasonic arms around. She waited for it to happen. The Change she'd heard about. The wonder—if that's what it was—of seeing the living thing inside you for the first time. But she found it hard to define what the thing was just now.

If she felt something for the strange creature on the screen it could probably best be defined as sympathy. For the fact that it would be hers. But her overriding feeling was something entirely unrelated. It was, in fact, an almost unbearable need to pee—a result of the four pints of water they'd made her drink beforehand. Apparently the entire process wouldn't work otherwise. When people tell you stories about this moment in awestruck tones, she thought, they leave that part out.

Finally, the female handed her some paper towels.

"You might want to clean yourself up. So I'll see you again for your next scan in about two months. Is there anything you want to ask?"

"No. Nothing. Thank you." As she made for the door, she gave what she felt to be a smile.

*

In the months he'd stayed, he painted the walls of her house with murals depicting what she took to be sea creatures of some kind. Bright turquoises, corals, and yellows, and other colors she didn't even have names for. She let him because she found she liked the novelty. Each evening she would step inside to be greeted by new colors and the smell of spices from the kitchen.

But he shed on the sofa. And he was over-affectionate. At times she would be working and he'd come up beside her to rest his head on her knee. The unaccustomed everyday closeness of it always made her jump and look down, as though seeing him for the first time.

Sometimes he would disappear with his rucksack for two or three days at a time, and reappear with money. This he would spend on fresh supplies of functional lager, more paint, unusual foodstuffs and guitar picks. On one return he produced a bag containing two kangaroo steaks. Once she'd looked into his rucksack out of curiosity. It contained a few spare clothes and an ancient alarm clock.

In the evenings he played his guitar. Or he would tell her stories about people he knew from "back home." She only half-believed him.

*

And then one day she left work to find him playing his guitar on the pavement outside her office. She'd pushed open the stubborn double doors and he was floating on air. She blinked with shock at the sudden brightness and the way the early evening winter sun lit him like a hovering miniature Jesus. Then she realized he was standing on a see-through plastic box.

"What are you doing?"

"I wanted to come and see you."

"Are you drunk?" She looked around for empty cans.

"No, I'm not. Come and stand up here with me and sing." He strummed a few chords.

"I've had a really terrible day. I want to go home. Everyone I work with will come out soon and they don't want to see us singing on a box like a couple of bloody hippies."

"I've never met anyone you work with."

"No, well you wouldn't like them. They're normal."

"Are you angry I'm here?"

"You're everywhere."

"What do you mean?"

She looked away from him in case he was wounded. Squeamish.

"I can't keep you in my house anymore."

"But we've been happy."

"But it wouldn't last would it?"

After that there was little more to be said. Later on he took his guitar and rucksack and left. It was only afterwards it occurred to her that she had no way of finding him, supposing she wanted to. No phone number. No address. No last name. Not that she did, of course. Want to find him.

And then even later she found that something was growing inside her. She came to the conclusion that life was nothing more than sudden leaps and awkward landings.

*

It had been too early, the day she'd sat in the waiting room. When they called her name it wasn't even light outside, not properly. And she'd been drifting in a vortex of sleep and nausea. It had been snowing for the past hour.

As they went through the double doors, she passed a teenager with what she assumed were her parents. Eyes cast down with a beaten-dog expression. A middle-aged woman with a friend saying, "I've already got four to take care of. I can't be doing with any more."

And now she was sitting in a small room facing a hospital employee of some kind. She might have been a doctor. Maybe she hadn't said.

"Are you certain you want to do this? You still have time. It's still quite early." Her voice contained an edge of disapproval, or possibly it was weariness.

"I am." She was.

"Then you'll need to go through and talk to the anesthetist as well so they can explain what will happen."

But even as she heard the words and nodded, something unexpected was happening. Tears spurted from her eyes and she watched, outraged, as they fell down her front.

The woman pounced. Saying something about her needing more time to go away and "really think." But she was too alarmed at this manifestation of apparent distress to listen properly. Because inside there was no feeling that she could identify. No need, in fact, for that anesthetist and their needle. Was this how it would be from now on? Body and mind conspiring against her?

"But I don't want to have a baby. I've never even held one before. I wouldn't know what to do with one."

The woman shook her head. "I'm sorry. I don't feel it would be right for us to perform the procedure today. You're quite obviously upset. Maybe you should speak to someone. I can arrange that if you'd like?" She brushed this off with a short wave of her hand. An abortive attempt at control.

"No. I don't need to talk to someone."

"But you do need to go away and consider this a bit more. I take it you have somebody to come and collect you?"

"Yes. Yes, of course."

Breathing deeply, she walked unsteadily back through the swinging double doors. As she stepped outside into the snow her mind ran over how she would get home. Bus? Taxi? Walk? What would she do? Eat? Sleep? Gaze at the wall? She decided to walk. She made several miles of heavy black imprints in the snow from the hospital to her front door. She stopped once on the way, to buy some paint.

She'd been told to think about "it" but found herself unable. Somehow during that long walk home, a wall had been constructed inside her brain around those specific thoughts. And whatever had put up that wall had placed a sign outside saying *Nothing To See Here*.

Instead, she found herself recalling how on more than one occasion people had described her as "brittle."

"You can be a very brittle person," they'd say. Were they implying that she was hard? Or something else?

*

She felt no sense of missing him in the months that followed. She knew in any case that her friends had vaguely disapproved of his presence in her life. And so she stopped mentioning him. Did they even know what he looked like? How his hair grew in matted curls of black and grey? She didn't want them to see her now anyway, because really there was nothing to see. As her insides shifted to make space for what was inside her, she grew bigger. And the bigger she got, the less of her there was. Until today, finally, she was uncertain whether she had ever been anybody at all.

Yes, she knew all these things, but she couldn't feel them. The numbness from that morning in the hospital remained with her. And now she sat by the lake and waited for reality to untether itself. If she were to reach out with both hands she could tear apart this picture of the water and the long grass and the insects and the sky. There would be a black space behind it for her to fall into, like an empty womb.

At the other side of the lake the flat, dry landscape stretched for miles. There was a person walking but they were too far away to see who it was. Could it be him? No, of course not. He had gone back to wherever it was he came from. And even if it were she knew he wouldn't leap across to join her. Fuck you. She said it out loud.

But was she, somehow, carrying this living thing around inside her in order to keep some gossamer-thin thread attaching her to him? She imagined, suddenly, that wherever he was he would one day feel a pull from this invisible thread. Was this thread a form of apology for her shortcomings as a person?

She hoped she would like the creature inside her. She hoped it would not be like her. She hoped, in fact, it would be another manner of being altogether.

It was only when she stood up, finally, to go. It was only then that the pain hit. And it rooted her. And she was glad.

How Deep

TONI LA REE BENNETT

How deep
        is the impression
                my body makes
                        in your wife's bed?

Third Eye Darkly

KEVIN McLELLAN

Last night in the boat their

mouths mouth *O God O*—
Mother Craniata stopped

egg laying upon sensing
extinction—and their why

-oh-why-am-I-body? pupils!

Papa, Too

BRITT HARAWAY

As Ashton was in the middle of drinking one night, he found himself in the kitchen carving a slice of watermelon for his child instead of pouring one from the fifth. She'd asked so sweetly for the fruit that he felt guilty. Guilty for the few times he must have snapped when pulled from his life by her wishes.

Through training, he'd strewn imaginary alarm bells around his easy chair that his family knew about and he liked them there. They kept his ex-wife in another room on the other side of town, her good cheer wrapped up around some other man. They kept his mother off the phone or whittled her down to just a few questions, mostly about the girl, how their weekend had gone, and if the money had arrived.

Hearing his daughter's soft voice say "watermelon" hadn't been part of the night's plan. He'd bought it at the farmer's market two weeks earlier, one that set up near the park with the ducks that they liked to feed. And he'd promised to open it that day, but instead forgot it in his car. The problem with watermelons is that they are unpredictable. It's just too much juice. It's ridiculous really. They just keep feeding these melons water like crazy and the next thing you know your floor is sticky, and your wrists, and your kid has it all over everywhere.

But she remembered. So Ashton was carving out a big slice for her like a long smile, and the knife felt good and easy going in. He was putting the slices on a paper plate and she was clapping and jabbering and then looking up at him like it was he that had done something. He wanted to tell her about his past, about the thousand mistakes and lost chances, and also about the laziness. And she thought he'd made watermelons.

"Papa has some. Papa too." Alice was a weird kid. She was always wanting you to participate in something good she was doing. Her mother had been like that too.

And there was no saying no. He'd forgotten about the great mix of watermelon. How the juice is there but with the crunch too, and how most often things just go soggy in all that wet but the melon somehow keeps its significance. It is nothing and it is a flood and it also has density and destiny. A grainy texture that stays on your tongue. And the nice resistance and sound as you chew that he'd felt when he sliced it up.

It was something, the look Alice had given and all the rush of sweetness of the melon, and it could have been that he had not had water that whole day, except for the slow ice melt that watered down the bourbon, but whatever it was, he'd not needed anymore liquor that night. And when he put his head down on the pillow it just sank all the way to the mattress and that was it.

ALEX DREPPEC

EXOPLANETIN   EXOPLANETRESS

Nach der Radialgeschwindigkeitsmethode.
Ich analysierte deine Atmosphäre *(wer pflügt deine Äcker?)*
beim Transit vor einem anderen Stern *(du entfixt deine eiernde Mutter)*,
dessen Licht dadurch einknickte.
Als es deine Lufthülle durchdrang,
schicktest du dunkle Linien in meine Richtung.

> By the radial velocity method.
> I analyzed your atmosphere *(who plows your fields?)*
> while you were transiting another star *(you dislocate your wobbling mother)*
> whose light therefore dimmed.
> When it penetrated your atmosphere,
> you were sending dark lines in my direction.

Deine Volumenprozente: Your percentages by volume:
    77,6 % N2,   21,3 % O2,   0,5 % Ar,   0,3 % Kr.
Spurengase: Trace gasses:
    CO2 0,1 %,   CH4,   O3,   SO2.

Nahezu außerirdisch.   Almost extraterrestrial.

Nun weiß ich: du bist in der habitablen Zone.
Da ist eine Biosphäre *(wer pflügt deine Äcker?)*
und ich *(du entfixt deine eiernde Mutter)* werde sie nie sehen.

> Now I know: you are within the habitable zone.
> There is a biosphere *(who plows your fields?)*
> and I *(you displace your wobbling mother)* will never get to see it.

Bedridden

ARIEL DAWN

Mice eat through walls, spring-loaded traps; their mouths make hallways. I hold my breath and bed rails, so rib bones whiten and display my cage. I'll eat inside out until walls collapse and I rise, a shadow.

By the glass doors a saucer of milk for the cat who sleeps in the hollow of my belly. She's late. I lose my breath—heart caught like dust in a windy shrinking room, soul a cigarette.

I see her in the fog. She won't look at me or the milk. Last time I closed all doors and windows and found her clawing at the wall in the morning: she looked wild, a hunter.

Crying from One Eye

CATFISH McDARIS

Smoofy sold a mixture he called weed,
he started with some high grade Mexican,
breaking up all the shake, tops, seeds and
stems, then he'd mix in about half catnip

He used a Mr. Coffee grinder on the stems
making them rollable, then he'd fill baggies
with shake, stems, catnip, seeds, and three tops,
his lids looked good and weighed one ounce

Smoofy was my best friend growing up, I was
making a living off the five finger discount,
there wasn't much I hadn't stolen, we were
quite the rip-offs, when the cops took Smoofy

My entire world collapsed, darkness smothered
the sun strangling the light from the sky, when
I visited him in Santa Fe in prison, I asked him
if he needed anything and he said, "Never trust

the candy man, his treats will make your teeth
get rotten and fall out and beware of losing touch
from not touching, women that cry from one eye,
sometimes the happy ending is at the beginning."

Damn Skippy

JEFFREY CYPHERS WRIGHT

The teepee's not big enough for everyone.
Why don't you just go buy something?
I would be a penguin in hell
and spit at the inferno. By your leave.

Cut me. Wound me. Do your worst.
In the notched announcement pod.
In the vanish drift of cooked north.
Chopping through the language glut.

If it would keep you from mugging yourself.
Sun Lord. Here is my HELP sign.
Would you rather do the frog walk
Or the perp march? This is only a test.

Even if you stand on a deserted speck.
Hacking the floor with a speckled axe.

Lindsay Spanish

PETER C. SWINBURNE

Lindsay Spanish took her tits to the chiropractor to get em reset. They'd been "off" for a couple weeks, Desmond told me, and it was upsetting him.

"It's like they're lookin at me funny. Or like they just had a stroke or somethin. Good pair of tits like that, it's a damn shame. She oughtta take more care of em. I had a rack a lumps like that, I'd buff em every day, put lotions on em, make em feel special. I wouldn't just let em get all rumpsy-tumpsy like that. Like they're avoiding each other. Like the left one was a little drunk and it made a joke that was kinda racist or somethin, ya know, misjudged the atmosphere, and the right one got a little offended, and the left one's embarrassed, lookin down at its shoes, and the right one's lookin off in the distance, pretending it wasn't even really listening, tryna kinda save face for the left tit.

"But it's like, Lindsay, she don't give a shit. Like she got a couple Ferraris and she just leaves em out in the driveway to get birdshit on em and the kids run their scooters into em and dent up the fenders and shit like they're some fuckin second hand '94 Ford Taurus with old french fry smell and stains from when the kids dropped their applesauce and shit and she just doesn't give a fuck because she's tired. The fuck she's so tired about? Stayin at home all day, watching her fucking cooking shows, decorating shows, smokin cigarettes, readin those sackashit Queen Elizabeth mommy porn books and pretending like she's learning all about history, calling up fucking Carol and yapping about Christ knows what for hours on end.

"I fucking work for a living. She twiddles her thumbs up her twat all day and says she's too fucking tired to take care of her tits, her one fuckin, her two fuckin saving graces."

"Mm," I agreed.

"There's one thing," Des said, "There's, there's two things, just two things I'm looking forward to when I come home at the end of the fuckin day, and it's not my fucking kids, know what I mean."

"You mean your wife's tits."

"I mean my wife's tits. And when I been busting my ass for nine hours with Peters yelling down my fuckin throat the whole time, and I get back and take my shoes off, all I want to do is bury my head in a good set of tits."

"Yessir."

"And I want the tits to welcome me. I want em to say, 'Come here, Desmond! Stay awhile! Make yourself comfortable! Put your feet up!' Instead, I got the one saying, 'Desmond, let me press myself right into your ear, nipple-first, and tell you all about my day. First of all, Lynette called me to ask if I'd seen her casserole, and that fucking bitch, it's like she was accusing me, she's always had it out for me because I'm prettier and she's jealous and . . . ' and the other tit is like, 'Fuck this, I'm outta here.'"

"Hm," I said.

"So I told her to go to the chiropractor, get em sorted out."

"Chiropractor do tits, or . . . ?"

"Yeah, he'll do tits. I know the guy. He'll do tits."

Anyway, so she went and got her tits did. Then I come round couple days later to return their leafblower. And Lindsay answers the door, cigarette inner mouth, says Des ain't there. Kids ain't there either, school I guess.

"Can I ask your opinion about something," she asks me, "do these look straight?" and she rips her fuckin top off, no brar unner it, just her tits.

And I say, uh, "Yeah, Miss, they look pretty straight to me. Lemme get a closer look though so I can make sure." These are good tits, ya see. These are tits you can bounce a quarter offa. You can put just one of em on your back and feel like fuckin Atlas with the ball there. You can frame these tits and put em in a museum.

So she takes me inna the kitchen where she's baking. She kneels down and lays her tits on the counter and I get up close and inspect em, feel em up with my hands, work em like dough. "Yep," I say, "these are tits alright."

"No," she says, and she takes the spatuler and the bowl she's workin with and she starts spreadin this fuckin icing all over her tits. She says, "They ain't tits. They're pies."

Minute later I'm fuckin Lindsay Spanish over the kitchen counter. She answers the phone when we're still going at it, but I mean, she keeps going, I keep going, whatever, no big deal. And then she just starts screaming! And I'm like, fuckin A, I still got it. But it turns out that was the call from the police tellin her how Desmond just got killed out onna freeway. But I can't hear it, so I don't know this until after we finish, and then she's just screaming and going hysterical, and I don't know what the fuck to make of this. Shit, still don't.

But anyway when we were banging there was all this icing flying off her tits from the centri . . . the centripa . . . from her tits flopping up and down, right? And I looked at the floor and up the wall, and I noticed . . . all that icing her tits had flung off? I shit you not, two perfect parallel fuckin lines.

Guy did a good job.

Point

BRIAN SHEFFIELD

Point:
- It isn't real if you can touch it.
- It isn't real if you can breathe it.
- It isn't real if you can fuck it.
- It isn't real if you can conceive it.

In the realm of this imagination
When every light has fallen from its source
Like the shards of a bulb leftover on the linoleum floor
There is only point and point and point.

Point:
- There is no such thing as oxygen
- Thetre is no such thing as chlorine
- There is no such thing as Styrofoam
- There is only light and dopamine

I thought I awoke from the sleep of day
And crawled with the thick hair of my gut
Into the dark mouth of my mother's breast
To drink deep from her drying well
Like a drunk thirsty for a new glass of cheap beer.

But the legs of chairs are like the hairs on a spider's limb
And the old words scratched on the round surface of a new dinner table

Reflects a mythology of knights now brought to the earth
And replaced with a loss of instinct and the perversion of conductive metals.

Point:

- It isn't wrong that I am afraid of mushrooms only because of the prospect of shitting alone.
- It isn't wrong that I question urination when I'm high.
- It isn't wrong that my lungs can't hold as much air since I've started smoking cigarettes and pot again.
- It isn't wrong that I want more than acid eyes.

Wen brane kemistrie is aulterrd en such u drastik waie that thot paternz moov frum u priscribed lojik tuu an inventd sents ov realitie in soe much that habbit and epistamolojy must be rekunfigured, tyme, 4 thoze momints, becums enkonsiquenchal, and thuss, seesis to eksist.

Point.

Information

BOB HEMAN

There were stories filled with frogs that traveled faster than the bears. In each town the bears visited, at each inn and stable, they heard only about the frogs, and what they had done there only a day or two before. The bears had never seen the frogs, and it seemed unlikely they would ever catch up with them. What they did not know was that behind them, a day or two behind them, there were foxes who heard stories each time they stopped, stories about themselves, about the incredibly hungry bears who never seemed to pause on their unexplained journey.

échappé

BRI ONISHEA

             we tiptoe
backward
          on the
                 balls
          of our feet,
ballerinas abandoning grace and
                              convention
pirouettes,
          you tell me,
          as you lace your slippers up to
          the palms of your hands,
are overrated

                    style,
               you insist,
is a black square to the white
                    the anti-hero
          deflowering the virginal maid

i'm intimidated by your made-up
          nutcracker face
your mouse-king eyes
          can't help but find swans
                    in your *soubresauts* and

attitude devant,
long for wings in the way you dance-defy the sugar plum fairy
and her *pas de deux* with princes

sometimes i wish i wasn't
captivated
by your spun-sugar words
sickly purple like your swollen tongue

travel to before
the land of sweets when
i was clara waking up beneath the christmas tree,
open my eyes to red orange yellow green
lights and pine needles in my palm,
instead of under the barre with runs in my tights

ruined last pair of snow-white

Nightfall

ELIZABETH ROSNER

The moon is knocking on the high window
                a dog is barking at the darkening sky   a child
is shouting No to the dog and the moon   I am losing
                the light   the trees are losing their color on the crest
        of the mountains under the knocking moon
                        the barking sky the darkening dog and the light saying
No to my hand   as the man next door says I can't I can't

        And now that the dark is falling he has finally stopped
                running the train in his backyard   no more whistle
rush of wheels   no more conducting the twilight

        The man shouts Hey Jody bad dog   and the child says
                Daddy he didn't mean to   as the moon knocks louder
and the sky comes closer to the trees   everything loses
                its outlines   and my hand keeps shouting in the dark

BOB HART *was born in Harlem in 1931. He served in the army from 1952 to 1954 and was stationed in Germany during the Korean War. Later, Bob hitch-hiked across the United States, studied art, worked for a mail sorting company, and renewed his high-school love of poetry. Many of us at great weather for MEDIA first met Bob on the New York City open mic circuit in the 1990s and 2000s at venues such as ABC No Rio and The Cornelia Street Café. He was the author of two collections of poetry:* Acrobat *(Words & Pictures Press, 2001) and* Lightly in the Good of Day *(Bench Press, 2010). Bob passed away in August 2014. Here, Bruce Weber—founder of The No Chance Ensemble performance group of which Bob was a member—gives a tribute to our much-missed friend.*

Breaths   In Memory of Bob Hart

BRUCE WEBER

Fairyland was an alternative universe for Bob. A land distant from the earthly ground we toil on in the heat of the sun. Populated by playful creatures turning in the light of the supernatural. Bob was always looking for the supernatural to intervene in the common day. Bob leapt on the back of fairies. Lingered in their fields. Embraced them in his poems and gave them life. He understood the mind is a portal that can carry us on long journeys where the impossible is as transparent as glass.

Bob would sometimes sit in the dim of the morning light with a pen in his hand and a sheet of white paper writing a poem. He often had an amused expression on his face—as if he was playing a game of catch-as-catch-can with fate and destiny and the crossing of swords of pirates in some tale of ancient glory and woe. As a child, he loved Howard Pyle and searched everywhere for anything he illustrated. Pirates and fairies unlocked some secret chamber in his brain where day and night mingled and opened the flood gates of his imagination. This was an unusual place: Bob's imagination. Filled with things that enchanted him and that he embraced fully. Bob's unwavering attachment to those things was his strength and originality. Bob steered his own course in the dark / on wavering seas / in the midst of any tumult.

Bob liked periods. He had a special way of placing them at the end of words to emphasize where he wanted a pause/a breath/a deep inhalation. These pauses in language permitted the poem to breathe. An intricate dance of elbows and knees and footsteps. Everything went into setting up the final words. A resting place for the soul. A summing up of a particular universe. When Bob, my wife Joanne, and I collaborated on the writing of our experimental non-narrative three-part *Belinda and Mark* series, we allowed spaces for the other writer to come in and detour the absurd shenanigans of the poem. Sometimes Joanne pulled in the reins so one might imagine a narrative where one simply did not exist. Bob would throw in an exclamation point of a poem. A loud burst of squeaking cars and artful alibis. Of tender mercies and irreverent leaps onto rooftops. He was travelling light years ahead of the poem. Flashing teeth and permitting the words to jump out like sparks. Then we'd gather up all the poems and create a fluid dance from section to section/ allowing the elbows to jut out/making no apologies for loose limbs.

One night in the woods, Bob looked up at the sky full of stars and stood there transfixed by the glimmering. Naming constellations. Pondering the ineffable. Joining the dots of Orion. Lost in the matrix of distant suns. In the morning he sat on the porch writing a poem about the ceiling of the sky while deer crossed the road and cats prowled in hopeful quest of sleeping birds. I watched as Bob captured the heat of the world on the page till it started steaming like an old locomotive. I watched as Father Time clinked his weary bell. As the Milky Way sped across the sky in a *pas de deux* with the keeper of the keys. Bob dashed off a line as Venus erupted from the stream and Acteon watched as her beauty unfurled into the day and Bob just sat there and laughed and laughed and laughed.

Once I spent a day with Bob at the museum. Chasing butterflies in a pastel by Redon. We discovered one sleeping on the skin of a woman in a painting by Titian and watched the butterfly examine every frame of her skin like a camera. Bob caught every butterfly and let them fly free. In front of the Fra Angelico, Bob got down on one knee and praised beauty like the true Keatsian he was. When we entered the room with the Turner marine of a phosphorescent golden sea, everything went still. It was as if the moon had entered the room through a side entrance and the sky was filled with the melodious sound of a whip-poor-will. Later that afternoon, Bob took out a pair of white leather gloves and performed magic tricks in front of the Duchamp. I watched as a parade of hats grew out of the spokes of a bicycle and a large mirror reflected back the past. Bob turned his face toward the light streaming in from the ceiling of the sky and reveled in the afternoon sun.

Make Such Pretty

BOB HART

Who knows how many worlds
have been ground into detritus
but they make such pretty stones.
One can collect them for
their sparkles or
their dullish characters;
ably make fairy tales about them;
wear them as
a savage wrapping around the
wrist or
round the loins; bed them
in a chapel floor or cavern's copula;
press their patterns into flesh
as fashion or as torture;
grind out one's eyes with them as guilty;
give them as worth
and still not guess
the distances they came from—
the processes that formed them.

The Amys Apologize

AMY WRIGHT

Dear ghost moose, whatever we do—assuming we choose
to act, or react,
won't reinstate your glossy

hide. Hoary and grizzled with tick-bitten patches,
your tattered coat goosepimples Amys all over
Minnesota and out-of-state Amys where moose are not

"on the way out."
Whether shorter winters and hotter summers
manage parasites poorly or compromise more

well-insulated creatures' immunity
is indeterminable. Snowslide-
steep decline, though, is certain, forcing

Chippewa tribes to scrap hunts, as brain worm
populations fatal to moose rise. News-knocked
Amys count not in the 97.5% dieoff

nor time lost picking her selves up.
But legions of Beloveds, betrothed, single, bibliophilic,
wingéd and bang-less

draft far-ranging missives. Forgive us
our daily deli sushi trip carbon emissions.
We are compensating

for audience-applauded pageants, wage gaps, glass ceilings,
unsuperlative high school yearbook pictures,

ankles tube socks cannot thicken.
You bear our weak spots, freak shows.
Pattern baldness spreads like housing

developments. Civilization's waistline displaces
dwarf-birch forests. Apoplectic Amys in electric hatchbacks
barrel over past-bog zones, stitch recycled-floor-mat moose

turnouts, eat Tofupups© in your honor,
bedraggled Bullwinkle, if research deems such gestures useless.
We jumping-jack up our couch potato buttocks,

palms smacked overhead, televisions berating
us sweating on the floor—pathetic even, skin weeping
tears our eyes refuse to shed.

ghost train or fun house given the choice you choose
slot machine   leave an indelible print in the sand
man's face   shriek "tooth fairy do you want
some   rip van winkle gonna fuck you up
son"   type who emerges from disciplinary
hearings with reputation enhanced   welcome to
integrity   could battle grunts not be harmed   then
the heavens opened we proportioned blame to both
the music industry & the government   but terminal 4
glory hole you scuttled me with gag scuttled me with
gag slain me with
laughter   dry stuff this eve if
an invisible man scrawls invisible ink all over
our apartment wall do we still get our deposit you
ask they listen to you   white dome islands you promised
me digital native i
was in margins with green
men   now i filter your
antics like brine through
an oyster i take the good bits

Queen Vic

ROBERT GIBBONS

he fondled her breast in front of us
all the rest of the boys engaged
at the bar with talk about their trips
the psychedelic of the east village
the need to get laid near the couch
made of old stories and cruising
glory holes and choosing
the tease pleases his testosterone
with the air of bourbon and vintage ladies
made the evening interesting

the word was still pending
how far will they go as we watch
the show, but the night drags
smokes in a double entendre

and you, with hetereo tendencies
should come hear the reading, queerly
having to deal with your broken marriages
and dysfunction, did I say oral
yes, oral interpretation;
yes, fellatio of the orifice, a divorce
from the establishment and this
is not gratification as he fondled her

breast pointing his phalanx towards me
as if he wanted me too
know a boy with dirty fingernails
as I tried to finish the sentence
but there are straight blocks,
more of a fag than a hag.

Injectable Tigers

DEBORAH STEINBERG

Tigers do not differentiate between the inside you and the outside you. Tigers strike through: ~~mate, lover, healer, artist, traveler, parent, divining rod.~~ Strike through all receptacles for fitting what shouldn't be fit into what is ill-designed for fitting. Tigers do not fit into receptacles other than veins.

How to pierce the night tiger? How to pierce the outer tiger without spearing the inside ones, the tiny ones?

A cutlass to beat back the grasses. A cutlass to spear the tiger lurking in tall grass at the back of the yard. The dream tiger come to devour. Perched on the fence. Immune to the dream. Immune to the drug. Immune to the rogue immune system.

Feeling only its tiger-ness and the tightness of the feeding tube. Tiny tigers traveling in vital spits of vicious liquid. Tiger injector punched directly to bloodstream.

Rogue cells roar and flare, disappear, devoured. Teeny tiny tigers tearing up the blood, devouring the devourers inside.

Ravenous with tiger hunger. Inside tigers ripping disorder to ribbons. Outside tiger perched to pounce. Constricted and constrained for our own safety. So they can tear us, so we can tear, but not entirely through.

My Whole Eye Was Sunset Red

ALAN GINSBERG

My whole eye was sunset red.

Back then when my face
kissed the bricks, the boys made it
kiss concrete and their boots
kissed me all over and anxiety
fell in love.

Friends say who dunnit
they say call the coppers
say po-lice will help
bad seeds don't grow in no
fertile soil
dey say dey all bad seeds
in my neighborhood.

Don' matter on a Son day
don' matter if your son's dey
don' care if they hit suns.

Do we question the squirrel's
fast ascent
home?

My whole eye shifts moon phases.

Now Safeway is dangerzone
my name, easy target
target practice outta convenience
since when were groceries
a contact sport?

Auntie tries to contact the ghost
of your bruises,
            tries to connect the pattern
of your abuses,
            tries to stop talking about the pain.

An expectant child believes
the purpose of pigeons
is to fly
when we get too close.
I am without wings.

Gail tell me they say house catch fire
tell me they say house gone
            no home // scorched earth
Gail say they burn down 'fore eviction

say fire cleanse better than the boots.

say fire, say fire, say fire

Gail tells me not to question
our purposed encounters

that there is a lightness
in our
humble meeting,
       an urgency in our stardust collisions.

Collision with another star doesn't
snuff out
       your light.

My whole eye burns like dawn
       says burns kiss away
       all the traumas
              but they still here though.

Harlem, U.S.A.

CHRISTOPHER J. GREGGS

In the forgotten silence of the East,
the slums hum from the street corners
a Lexington prayer for the whales
in our beds.

At the franchise chicken-box
on 125th Street & St. Nicholas,
a starving-god sells to us a slave
painting and opens our door.

"Do not lose your thread.
The world is full of people,"
he warns.

In the summer we commit
to the philosophy of strolling
past the drummers,
in front of the Adam Clayton Powell
State Building—where Father-Heron
sings from vendor tables
of Grandma's Hands.

"My brother's a junkie—
said he ain't got no job,"
he adds.

In my room, I read, and the silent
phone does not hurt as much.
I dream of women with no faces—
their asses on their shoulders,
and Coltrane winds that strike
the harpsichord—a gypsy move,
and flow over the upward tacks
on God's floor, while the school children
walk on eyelids to watch the bums
age to glorious bone in the cut
of Broadway and the Projects
of Moylan Place.

Here's the Real News

JON SANDS

The hurricane hits Brooklyn this weekend
two days ago an earthquake shook down Manhattan
and no one got hurt but a few people felt dirty
and if it is true that this year tucks the apocalypse
in its knapsack and if it is true that our eyes
look over our shoulders until we smack into
something big and if it is true that a human being
is alone in the universe then why do I need to wait
to start getting busy? I mean no disrespect
I need someone to gift wrap the goodies
set them down and then stay and I am not talking
about sex but I am not not talking about sex.
I have kicked through enough doors to know
when I'm not doing shit and this isn't about fear
but it's not not about fear—this poem is going
to manifest me I can feel that so I am writing it
fast on the Manhattan-bound A train
begging this dude in the newsy hat, mustache,
and coffee thermos to tell me to stop
so I can snatch one of his chucks and throw it
through the closing doors at High Street I am
begging my man in steel toes across the aisle
coming off the graveyard shift arms tight
crossed asleep like this is a crib to hand me

a sticky note that just says nah, so I can pack
it up for good and take the Midwest by storm
it doesn't always feel good to know what
you are and I am dangerous here and I am
vain today like my heartsong is on loop
through everyone's iPod buds and I am so
white like rice milk in rice pudding over a bed
of sticky rice like my ears are concrete like
my problem is on everyone's to-do list I am
running away from my bedroom because that
is where I keep me and I can't see me like this
with the suburbs on speed dial making some big
deal of every thought I can't think of this poem
like it's not me like it's not shook by a mirror
like it's not begging me to start some shit so it
can jump back into my face or leave.

Blind Gallery

JOSEPH KECKLER

My friend gets a travel grant and leaves town. I take over some of her shifts, working for a blind gallerist on the Lower East Side. He's not one of those blind people who you forget is blind. He won't let you forget. He begins every few sentences, "Now, I don't know if you know this, but I'm blind . . . " He is very erudite and with-it and his friends are always coming over to read him art reviews, the *New York Review of Books*, new poetry, new literature, on and on. But if you are me and you ask him "Say, did you read the such and such an article in the *New Yorker,*" he'll reply, "See, the thing is, Joe, I'm blind." Choking on laughter, he adds, "Can you imagine a blind motherfucker like me reading the *New Yorker* and some shit?"

My boss speaks through his teeth with a sense of strain and release, as though he is always simultaneously inhaling or exhaling a hit of pot. A breezy and hip walking bass drifts perpetually from the stereo behind him. He has a phone next to him and he makes calls all the time. But if the phone rings and I pick it up and it's for him and I turn to him and say, "Hey, so-and-so is on the phone," he replies, "I can't talk to him. I'm blind! Tell him I can't talk. He'll understand. He knows I'm blind." Sometimes my boss takes naps in the middle of the day. Sometimes, when the phone rings, he wakes up and picks it up and whispers, yawning, "Yeah, I'm in a meeting right now." When I ask him how he curates shows he mutters, "I got people I trust. I rely on their opinions."

I am quite diligent the day I start. Because my boss cannot monitor me—not visually, anyway—I don't feel rebellious like I do at other jobs. On the contrary, I feel a sense of honor and responsibility to take care of business with efficiency and care. When my friend calls him from out of town to see how things are going my boss says, "This Joe motherfucker is professional as shit. That motherfucker is pro- PROFESSION-al!AL." He deems me to be so professional that he soon decides to hire me on for a while. Even after my friend comes back to town I work shifts on the days she doesn't.

One thing I have forgotten to mention is that my boss' gallery is in his apartment. He sleeps on a couch in his living room. In the morning he wakes up and swivels his body, placing his feet onto the floor, and the setting transforms around him. Magically he is at work. Interns began flooding in. One intern. "Is fatso here yet?" my boss asks.

"No, not yet," I say. "She's not fat," I add, thinking that he might not know, since he is blind.

"Yeah, let's give fatso a call," he replies with a grin. "Let's get ol' fatso on the phone. See when she plans on, uh, rollin' on in here."

I have various duties. Sometimes I handle development. "Joe, can you call this rich motherfucker and see if he'll wire some money into our account?"

Other days I oversee marketing. "Joe, could you, uh, order a bike messenger? See if he can take this postcard invitation to our next opening up to Yoko Ono? I just heard on the news that she's back in town."

I also work in programming and one day my boss has a special mission for me. "Joe, listen. This friend of mine, a poet, uh, passed away." I nod solemnly, though my boss can't see me. "I mean this motherfucker just dropped dead," he continues. "So, uh, some of us are going to put on a memorial reading and we need a venue. So I'd like you to go over to the XYZ bar tonight and look into how we can book a reading. We just want to read some of this guy's poems since he just dropped dead on us, see." He feels around on the table for his checkbook, opens it, and scribbles out some numbers and loops. "I'll pay you an extra hour," he says, tearing out the check and handing it to me.

"Oh, thanks," I say, tucking it in the right pocket of my jeans.

"I'd go over there myself," he says. "But, you know, I'm blind."

First I try simply to find booking information on the website of the bar, which I knew to be a downtown destination of NYC literati. There are no instructions, just a phone number. I dial it. Nothing. So after leaving the gallery that evening I walk to the bar.

I climb a tall flight of stairs up to the second floor. I enter a dimly lit room. The air smells sick and sweet—the floor and tables are breathing into the room the stale vapors of years of spilt beers. A distorted, grungy bass line plays repetitively on the PA. A modest number of customers line the room, leaning against walls with their drinks, chatting in corner banquettes. The center of the room is empty.

A woman with messy jet-black hair sits at the bar, hunched over a half-drunk martini. She's got an unlit cigarette between her fingers. She conducts the air with it as she talks to the bartender. Occasionally she absent-mindedly draws it to her lips, before glancing downward and seeming to silently remind herself that in New York these days you can't have it both ways: no smoking inside, no cocktails on the street. I sit down at the bar, one seat away from her. The bartender is slender with a long pony-tail.

"What you want?" he asks me eventually.

"Hi," I reply cheerfully. "I actually just came in to get some information. I work for a gallerist, a blind gallerist, who is trying to organize a memorial reading for a friend of his—a poet who just passed away—and I need to know who I can talk to... about booking. A reading."

"Yeah?" the bartender says, lifting his chin, "Well I'm such a fucking bartender that all I can do is pour a drink." He turns and walks away from me.

"Can I get a gin and tonic?" I ask.

"Five," he says.

I slip him seven. "So is there a number or an email address that I can give to my boss?" I ask, adding, "I would really appreciate whatever you have." The bartender reaches for a book of matches, and tosses them at me. The XYZ phone number appears at the top.

"Thank you," I say. "But I already dialed this number and there was no ... info ... "

"Give it up!" The black haired woman laughs, tapping the filter of her unlit cigarette. My eyes follow imaginary ashes as they fall from the end of it into her now-empty martini glass. The bartender snatches up his shaker and refills her drink. "You're not going to win. Can't you see that?"

"Win?" I repeat. "I don't need to win. I just need to book the reading of a dead man's poetry. My boss would have come himself, but he's blind! You are such a 'fucking bartender', I understand that," I say, raising my voice as the bartender moves into the storeroom, out of sight. "And I bought a fucking drink from you. Now can you please let me know who I can talk to?"

After several moments the bartender reappears in the darkened opening of the storeroom. "Leave," he says. "You leave now."

He's got a vodka bottle in his hand. The woman leans on the bar with one elbow, and swivels to face me with a crooked smirk, twirling her now limp and wrinkled cigarette as though she's flashing a weapon.

"I'm not leaving," I declare. I am emboldened by duty, and also by gin. I am not here for myself—not here on my own time, my own dime. No, I am on the job. On the clock. The setting of work surrounds me like an aura. Furthermore, I am here as a representative of the dead and the blind. "If you want me to leave, you'll have to call the police and see if they can make me. I'm going to sit right here."

The bartender slams the bottle down. He reaches under the bar and presses a button. The music stops. Every head in the bar turns toward him, toward the two of us. He waits for a hush to come over the meager crowd before pointing at the door and shouting, "Get out now!"

I pretend not to have heard him. I become totally still. I say nothing. I just sit in my stool and stare blankly at the bottles in front of me. (They're arranged in tiers. They look like a senate of psychoactive beverages.) The bartender picks up the vodka. He walks out from behind the bar. He unscrews the cap. He takes a swig. He spits it back at me. It soaks my right shoulder and stings my neck. I don't move. He takes another swig and spits it at my face. I close my eyes. He circles me clockwise, continuing to fire 80 proof loogies from every direction.

Leaving the bar is not an option I consider. But how can I extract myself from what has become an unwitting piece of body art in which I allow this bartender to assault me with whatever he has on hand? Can I appeal to anyone in the bar?

As another jet of burning liquid grazes my left thigh, I instinctively slide my hand into my pocket in order to protect my cell phone. Suddenly it occurs to me—I could transport myself out of the bar without leaving. I pull out the phone. I flip it open and dial.

"It's Joseph. I am at the XYZ Bar."

"Oh yeah, Joe?" replies my boss, with a rasp. "You figure out how to get this memorial going? Tell 'em this guy just dropped dead."

"The bartender is spitting liquor on me." I state.

"Oh yeah? Spittin' on you? Well, Joe, those motherfuckers over there are crazy. That's all right. We don't have to do it over there. We can do it over at, uh, St. Marks."

With this pronouncement made, I no longer have business here. I return the phone back into my pocket, turn, and walk with matter-of-factness out the room, down the stairs, and out the door onto East 4th street.

I wander around the East Village, which is quietly bustling, alive with crepuscular chatter. I stop intermittently to sit on the stoops of strangers. I cook up plans. Revenge plans. Maybe I could return to the bar with a super-soaker squirt gun, I think. That'd learn 'im. And with which liquid might I fill it?

As the night air dries the liquor and saliva from my skin and clothes, my rage wanes. Eventually I resolve simply never to darken the door of the XYZ again.

The next morning I wake up. I reach over and pull the check my boss gave me out of my jeans. The numbers he wrote were already jagged and wild and now they're blurred from vodka. But they're still legible. I walk over to the bank. I deposit that check. It bounces.

JAY CHOLLICK

In Defense of Fear, Quivering, and Its Coward Sound

I think:
to soften horror; havoc;
or anything else
that smacks of it—I'll bring
to dynamite a tinge

Of pink; or perhaps, some
whip-lashed porno
shit. Would that repel the stiff-necked
mob? One hopes one almost
prays
it would

Or More Succinctly, in Defense of Cowardice

FOR SALE: Wax Wings, Used Once

LAUREN MARIE CAPPELLO

Into a country where stars remain
poised the soft shoulder & only light
travels o'er a slew of futures that
are not on time. A slew of futures
too late to happen. "I've outlived my
father in another way all together"
one thought.

But some are of similar clew
and privy to a bird's-eye view of a
small child adjusting the strap
of homemade wings, paternal
warnings fall like dew upon
grass & remain unabsorbed.

A child learns their imaginary
body like grown ups learn
heartbreak—lifting arms
to wind like addition, in the way
things become common sense
after long periods of knowing,
after long periods of forgetting
they had to be learned & had
to be taught enough for wind

to catch beneath them in the
rising crescendo of a kite
the rest of a weighted body
can take flight.

This is the unattestable secret
that remains in that malleable
cold earth like a crypt.

Dementia

MATTHEW HUPERT

Often @ loggerheads—
life taught you struggle & drive
honed you brilliant-sharp
& me ease and flow
easy slow and easy quick
still—too alike not to fight

I can't count the times
I'd wish you had a more Buddhist approach
that you'd divorce from
past pain and future fear
and live in the moment

But I didn't mean it like this
Now time's stripped from you
& this moment & this moment
& this moment & this
are all you are
& I'm so sorry mom
I didn't mean it like this

"whenever you fall i will be there to catch you"

AUDREY DIMOLA

curl around that space inside the word.
your face has become so dark, hollow.
the further you slip, drifting in your boat without oars, collecting stars—
still, i can see you.
still, i can reach you.
your pity for yourself feels inextricable.
your crash from the high, your bones made of pieces, somehow still holding in place.
i am holding that place.
i am watching you even through veils of darkness.
i am the breath that moves the curtain as you sleep.
that's all it is—
a curtain between these two worlds.
your life becomes a strange failure—
and you forget.
you don't want to be here anymore.
rooted to this pain,
guilt.
the thickness such that for once—
you can't cry.
and you still want to cry.
need to cry.
for her.
for him.
for them.

what about—for you?
all these curtains and boats and flowers.
be inside the curl of the word.
it is impossible to make light without shadow.
and so on and so forth—
you know this.
like your next breath—you know this.
i am the golden rim around the edge of asphyxiation.
the moment you see out of the corners of your eyes.
touch it—
you glow.
just when you think you can't breathe anymore—
the space in your ribcage opens to a canyon.
call your voice into it.
i need no offering but your unrest.
this moment, just as you are.
call your voice to me
up into the heavens you don't feel strong enough to believe in.
still, i can see you.
always—i will answer you.

Hoardin'

JENNIFER BLOWDRYER

It's interesting, for some reason, when the hoarders die upside down. How do they do it? I mean, we're all going to die, but we will most likely not be upside down at the time. That is so outta control. Hoarders, like the very fat, the very drunk, the very strung out, have clearly lost more than a margin of self-control.

They know they're doing something weird. Saving every back issue of *Cat Fancy*, every bank statement, bits of food, Styrofoam plates, unable to walk through their own domicile except through little paths that are known in the hoarder trade as Goat Trails. But they're OCD, so they keep right on piling stuff up, even though their respiratory system is trashed from the loads of dust, mold, and pet hair. Like smokers, they're crushing their own human lungs forever and for real. The pets who at least eat their carcasses have a little bit more joie de vivre, it would seem. Those pets want to LIVE.

Who doesn't? Get serious. Here's a government phone, call someone who cares! Good luck! I was sitting on a stoop in Glendale, California, because actually the cartoonist's place I was staying in (one door down from the Holy Roller and right next to the underground senior couple) was fairly filthy so I sat around in front a lot. Colleen, who was my hoarder for a while, came by the stoop with her little Alaskan dog (I forget the brand name) every night about seven. Neal, the ex-spook right next door, was usually out too. We were all in the bottom half of a beaten up non-earthquake proof building, whites at the end of our run.

The Scientology family upstairs, who we gossiped about to no end, fled in a van not long after Neal countered their mother's gift of a copy of *Dianetics* with a worn out second-hand, smoke-drenched edition of *The Book of Mormon*, just to mess with their heads. Men in suits came with a moving van and took them off to a far better place, while we remained with the San Fernando Valley quake-cracked terrace doors stuck shut, our weird piles of owning and being just Too Much. *No Justice, Just Us*, like the tattoo says.

This was the first little social group that welcomed me in my entire life. My cartoonist came out in the early evening with his ratty sweatshirt and jutting Movie Union Insurance mesh hernia sticking out beneath, and strummed some tunes on his geetar at night. Trevor, Neal's min pin (a non-wolf-descended alien little dog with skeletal limbs), might come out for just a few seconds and float around.

A woman walked by every night with her pug to say hello to Colleen and her Alaskan pooch. Not a bad social life, a regular cotillion. I never did meet a lot of people those years I spent propped-up in bed. At least I knew better than to have a pet around. Suicide. Vultures in fluff. They will eat a hoarder's corpse every time, the dogs waiting about a day or so longer than the cats.

Colleen has a greasy clump of short hair, huge breasts drooping under a housedress, and scuffs. She talks really really loud, which drives the Holy Roller next door crazy. Colleen's place was bad. She admitted this to me herself one day when we were hanging on the stoop.

"Maybe I can help," I answered.

"No, it's really bad," she clarified. Now Colleen became a challenge, a helper challenge, and I pressured her in a low-key way for days:

"Well, maybe one day you'll let me see!" I kept saying

I've got an eight-year-old girl and a spinster school marm that live in my vocal chords, and that's just two of them. There's a New Yorker, a Southerner, a Poor Person, a sing-song don't be scared of me middle-class voice beggar and opportuner, a crooner, and—dare I brag—a blueser. In addition, though I am moderate in my habits, I often sound flat-out drunk

Colleen did let me in one day, past the screen door. Oh my. The thing is to swallow your reaction, the first shock. When I was in the UK, a man at the local tube stop, face charred black from a fire, down to the skull, actually thought I was flirting with him. I was that good at suppressing a first reaction. Maybe I was just the only person who said hello as he haunted the train station. Lonely life. Expressing true shock is bad form. Fake shock is okay.

Colleen has empty boxes, bubble wrap, and ad hoc mobiles of shiny things placed non-strategically on every remotely high surface. She's got fake parrots and a steady wall of punishment color file cabinets, a white vinyl couch with no room to actually sit on in the living room area, and hundreds of pill prescription bottles that represent an imagined and hoped for meeting with a perfect doctor who will want to know every single detail of her prescriptionary past.

Hobbies they will take up one day is a big hoarder trait. Some of Colleen's interests and potential hobbies are: owning a parrot, returning to the work world by consulting ten-year-old newspaper classified ads, and maybe even using the five printers or several computer keyboard templates dating back from 1987. She also wanted to revise and sell a script Russ Meyer once expressed an interest in.

Colleen was also planning to make jewelry from hundreds if not a couple thousand gems, a project her and Neal had embarked on. Every pile is a project or a concept, unrealized, so putting a couple of issues of *Dog World* in a dumpster or sweeping a pile of change into just one baggy can break a hoarder, tear them right up. The type of dog on the cover of the magazine means something they might need to know, while the piles of change on dusty paper plates are, of course, organized by the state or the year or some damn thing. If you mess any of this up, their world is shattered and they will not let you, the destroyer, ever forget. The thought of the magazine back issue, the change, the tiny gem, runs through their brain like the worst kind of barbed wire prison. You must let them know that you know this. The big picture is you might be able to get rid of some of the Styrofoam but they, like the world, are not getting what an expert or landlord might refer to as Better.

Compounding Colleen's case was the shock therapy she herself had gone to the local hospital and demanded a decade or so ago. Sustainability doesn't work for medical treatment. "Think globally. Act locally" definitely should not apply to something so delicate as repeatedly zapping a person's cranium. Might want to shop around for that one. So sending her to, say, the other side of a Goat Trail with a garbage bag is not a real world scenario. She's gonna get stuck. Stand there with the garbage bag, brain cycling painfully.

It wasn't the worst job I ever had, crouching there with Colleen, living in her world, chiding, cajoling, and sharing. She liked me as well as the mentally ill can. Cautiously, now and then. I worked hard and actually got her to learn a new inner thought:

"Those products haven't existed for nine years!" I told her one day, looking at the dates on some of many mail order catalogue back issues. When I left, as one must, Colleen started looking at some of the catalogues I organized and telling herself, "These products do not exist!"

Did I mention you can break them? Well, they can break your heart too, when they do a thing like that. Still, I think that Colleen preferred to think of me as a type of coolie or brain-addled servant. It made the revelations less embarrassing.

On an Oprah episode, I'd seen the hoarder counselor ask this woman what she would ideally like her house to be. "A place my grandchildren can visit!" she wailed, sobbing.

I tried that with Colleen. "What would you like your apartment to be?" I queried.

"Well," she replied thoughtfully, "Somewhere I can display my stuff."

Hoarders can be cute. For two days, she got stuck on a weird Christmas display that could make a triggered holiday sound if all the cardboard and Styrofoam was working just right, and sat out on the top of her stoop tinkering with it for a few hours.

"When I was in group therapy, they told me to do one thing a day that makes me happy," she explained.

You go, Colleen. Like every artist in LA, she likes Christmas. A lot of the ones who live there have a little artificial tree that stays out for the whole year, choosing not to stash this most cinematic of holidays away in a closet for eleven months. Those people are at the end of the world, at least in terms of borrowing an item and returning it, keeping their word, having a conversation that doesn't connect to a labyrinth of connections real and hoped for. Right near the mythical screenplays you will always find a Christmas ornament, and I had a mythical hope of my own for Colleen, which was this:

Maybe her apartment could have every Christmas thing on display, ornaments, glitter, tinsel tin tree boas, the whole nine yards, and be a mini Santa Town visitors could enjoy. Not gonna happen. Like so many dreams, brothers and sisters. Anyway, are you perfect?

There is never a happy ending. As Steven Brown of Tuxedo Moon sings, "Sometimes I think that this short life . . . is just one long disease."

I missed a touching denouement, however, when Colleen dodged that big D Day for hoarders: eviction. Trumark Realty was going to send Jose over to see if there was any way to get to, say, a fire exit, or make an emergency repair, but of course they knew there wasn't. The building manager might as well have been checking to see if he could make it to the couch, which would have proved equally impossible.

Landlords and neighbors have a not irrational fear of hoarders. Cops and fire fighters will tell you that a hoarded place is like a bomb formula, layers of paper stacked in between bubble wrap, another of Colleen's favorite items. Fire catches rapidly and explosively. Therefore housing inspections and the resultant eviction are the most dangerous part of a pack rat's life.

My favorite term of landlord tenant law is "Notice to Cure" which can be used by either side. It's a "Cover Your Ass" notification of me telling y'all about the problem. Now if you don't fix it, the hammer's coming down hard and the housing court judge has no choice but to agree. My least favorite term dotting American right now is "Legally." As in, *You have to get your stuff and get out.* Legally.

Hoarder evictions are the reasons you see so many homeless wheeling around nonsensical items on purloined shopping carts. You know the look: stuffed animals, half a wrench, wrapping paper, all pouring out of the top and obstructing their own view of what might be coming up ahead, besides just the disdain of passersby

Conversely, impending eviction is really the only thing, besides maybe being in cognitive therapy every waking moment, that really motivates the hoarder. I sneakily called a company called Steri-Clean that served the San Fernando Valley area, and pushed Colleen on the phone with them. I felt hopeful, as she was on there for awhile, but then in retrospect she would talk to just about anybody about anything, including a free-floating sense of prejudiced indignation about the Cyrillic-using population that had quickly taken over Glendale.

"They were asking me the right questions" she reported of her Steri-Clean chat. One of them, apparently, was "Do you have a bathroom you are unable to use due to toxic waste?"

Why yes, yes she did.

"Do you have a pet and, if so, are there piles of animal fur everywhere?"

Check. She wouldn't go for the complimentary meeting with a counselor, though. At the time she trusted, unfortunately, only Neal and me.

When Colleen's D Day inspection came, Neal went to Home Depot, and gathered up five Mexican day-laborers. He arranged for storage space in a nearby garage, brought the men over to her place, and sat there holding her hand while the team carried out box after box to a truck Neal had amazingly also procured. Colleen cried, wept, shook, and took, no doubt, many pills, which is how they got through that earthquake of a day. She rightly tipped each man $60 to be part of a trauma.

Most people have a pack rat in the family or neighborhood back home. They know the deal. In this case, minimum wage and $60. Colleen passed her apartment inspection. She knew her things were safe. Neal knew that he and his wife were safe for a time because Colleen was covering their rent. I don't think Colleen, Neal, or definitely that ill wife of his are going to be around in, say, 2019, but the stuff will remain, long after our species suffers its lethal count down.

Let the dark water swamp our poisoned terrain as the Earth takes some time to detoxify, a quiet infinity, and Colleen's decorative crystals will sink down past the Styrofoam, soundless, as her leftover psychiatric medications leech through what's left of the soil, right past the sparkly yuletide greetings and dream catchers. It's possible Colleen, whose literary collection includes things people do in natural disasters, feels this at her very core.

A Poem Can't Start Like This

CRAIG COTTER

I had a 9 hook-up today for a half hour
could've been a 10 but had a barn-burner of a headache
that didn't end until the second hour of a foot rub
by Wan Ming Yang.
He is a 10.
3-day-old hickey on his neck.

If I didn't have that headache we could've gone an hour.
The poppers he used made my headache worse
(contact buzz).

*

Lovely Wan Ming Yang.
His slender fingers
rubbing my skull above my eyes
in the groove there.
The headache started to disappear the minute his slender fingers got in there.

*

Wan Ming Yang's ass goes on forever.
His waist is 29 inches.
You know when some guys are very young

their bubble asses are lifted—
the round part up by his back
then a steep rounding into the V as his crack disappears into his legs.
You just wanna get your hand in there.
Your tongue.

When he leans down I look in his t-shirt—
not a hair.
Flat stomach ripples as he bends.

*

I think Wan Ming Yang is lying on his side in bed lonely right now.
I think Alex is getting up to pee in New York at 4:16 a.m.

*

I thought in doing this
I'd remember two people.

Now, not only do I know nothing about them,
I can't remember them.

*

On the three wish dream
I usually want to know all the languages in the world.
Then unlimited money and eternal life.

*

You're a smart fucker reading this poem.
Of all the things you could be doing
glad you chose this.
Do you wonder what I was like?
Are you pissed that you didn't choose something else?
Do you feel you have to keep reading to see how it ends?

*

These great eternal questions. They really aren't questions. We hate the one answer
so we make giant buildings we don't let the homeless sleep in.

Unicycle / Tractor / Tennis Racquet

DOUGLAS COLLURA

I. When I was a kid, most of the neighborhood dogs passed away peacefully at home or quietly at the vet. My dog had the distinction of being run over by the only neighborhood dog that could ride a unicycle. It was trained by my next door neighbor who'd once been a professional clown and was maimed in the Great Clown Car Crash of '58, when two tiny cars stuffed full of twelve to fifteen clowns each collided on the L.I.E. Round red noses and large floppy shoes covered the roadway for miles. Broken-hearted bystanders laughed until they wept. It had left my neighbor a bitter clown. I'll never forget the smug look on his dog's face as it rode away, honking its little horn, smoking a cheroot. I gave it the finger. It gave me the paw. Stinking circus folk!

II. I hate leaving the city, but met a woman who invited me to her weekend place in the country. We walked in a neighboring field. "Doesn't that elm look like it's holding up the sky?" she said. "Are there ticks out here?" I said. "I don't want to get Lyme Disease." She climbed up into the cab of a rusty one-wheeled tractor. "Come on, let's have some tractor sex." "I'm phobic about one-wheeled vehicles." "Can't you be a real man?" "Hey, I hang out in the Village, read books, go to museums. Of course, I can't be a real man! If I could, I'd kick the shit out of you for asking." A farmer stepped out from behind an elm and said, "Out of my tractor, cookie, pronto." "I fear no one beneath me," she said, lifting her chin. He lifted his shotgun and blew her into a human dandelion. Uh, oh, I said to myself: A real man. He turned to me. "Are you with her, shorty?" He was actually shorter than me, but I kept that observation to myself. "I won't lie to you, mister. I don't know her from Adam." He fondled his rifle as I backed away slowly all the way home to 23rd Street.

III. Last week, Larry Kakowski, a poet known to so many of us here, died when he was run over by a dog on a unicycle. The fact that the dog was in the bicycle lane is little consolation. In keeping with the city's stringent animal control laws, the unicycle was put to sleep, and the dog was set free to kill again. Ah, justice. Ah, Larry. I first became aware of Larry's remarkable poetic abilities at the East Village Do Anything With a Ping Pong Paddle in Your Mouth Competition of '82. Most competitors did the obvious thing: played ping pong holding the paddles with their mouths. But Larry was too much the creator for that. He wedged the wide end of the paddle into his mouth and improvised his immortal poem *Ode to a Duck Billed Platypus*. I don't think any of us will forget the smile on his face that stretched from ear to ear literally, or the last couplet of his poem that became a downtown touchstone for years. I'll try to do it justice: "Whawooveselleainsaesisros / Whawooveselleaesquackquackquack." Words to live by. When it was announced that Larry had won the competition, his wife Edie, always his biggest fan, turned to the crowd and said, "You should see what he can do with a tennis racket." Now, we never will. Stinking circus folk!

Sun Net III

DEAN KRITIKOS

My speakers are broken   clicking
Then loud   they make the sounds they want
Nevermind the composition
Nevermind   once spontaneous solo

Made homogenous   eternal repetition
Pome breath   brush yr teeth
Yea I am
Books I will never read

Noam Chomsky is so ugly
My speakers click   my jaw
Clicks   the ceiling fan   wails
The air conditioner ought to be uninstalled

For winter;   I lack
what I want   but   am so spoilt otherwise

Flea Market Funeral

RYAN BUYNAK

never accept
an old espresso
from a lady named Karl
who sells shower heads
even if there is moonshine in it.

this place smells like wigs
and dresses are burning.

I buy pickles
from a Puerto Rican
thinking there is nothing more poetic
than walking around a dirt mall eating dills.

at the antique kiosk,
I buy an old pocket knife
that has RONNIE engraved
in the blade
and vintage Montreal postcards
that were filled out
and mailed in the 1940s and '50s.

I wonder how they ended up here.

I wonder the same about myself.

the proprietor of said shop
is a bald man with a glass eye
a grey beard
and a doubtless homemade leather Harley Davidson vest.
there is a fake-looking iguana on the cash register
yet I am startled when it jerks to life.
needless to say,
I am beyond surprised to find out
that it is real.

"chill out, Seymore!" the man says.
I choke on a laugh at the irony of the name.
the man looks at me like he knows what I am thinking
then I am even more surprised and startled when
the burly leather vested man starts crying
from his one good eye.

apparently Seymore had a brother
called Cyclops
who has just died.
just then the man reaches behind the counter
and produces a Payless shoe box.
he opens it,
and inside is a dead lizard.

how the hell do I get myself into these situations?

I am polite and I try to calm the
vested man down.
I just don't know what to do.
"when did Cyclops pass?" I ask.
"three weeks ago," he says through vested tears.

Now I am suddenly aware of the stench of decay.

without thinking
I say to the man
that we should throw a funeral party
for the long lost reptile.

of course, he agrees . . .

I run and get the pickle Puerto Rican
and the lady Karl
and a few other bystander babysitters
who doubtlessly
noticed the dead iguana in the box.

"this man needs us," I say
to the crowd of five or six or seven or four.
what's your name, sir?"
"Leslie," he says.
I didn't see that coming.
"Leslie, what would Cyclops have wanted?"

"well," he mutters slowly. "he would have wanted grass and dirt."
"great," I say, not knowing what else to say in the way of devils.

"well," Leslie slides. "I always used to walk him
behind the buildings in the St. Augustine grass on my lunch hour.
he seemed to like that."

so the shopkeepers put signs on
their posts that read in black
Back in 10 Minutes — *LIZARD FUNERAL*

and on our way out we pass a
corner hardware booth.
I buy a rusty shovel for five bucks
and invite the wayward Asian man of that
place to join us.
"what the hell," he says
and proceeds to follow.

outside, the air is heavy hot.
there is a small patch of grass
before a retention pond
and beyond that is a highway
cut off by concertina wire.

I dig a hole.
Leslie places the box in the hole.

I nudge Leslie to say a few words.

he is shy at first but then opens up.
he says something about how he has had Cyclops since
Hurricane Andrew "left him on my porch."
he is sincere
and he thanks the people around him.
Karl holds up her coffee cup and says "hear hear!"

then everyone walks away,
back into their lives, separated by
partitions and t-shirts,
and I am left alone with Leslie
and the shovel.

I hand Leslie the shovel
and tell him
to say goodbye to Cylcops.
He starts crying and covering the hole with dirt
and attempts the ashes-to-ashes-dust-to-dust recital bit
but messes it all up.

he eventually hands me the shovel.
he is done.
good for him.

and now I have a used shovel and a weird Florida folktale.

The Albino Watermelons

EDGAR OLIVER

An excerpt from Edgar Oliver's stage show Helen and Edgar *about his childhood growing up in Savannah, Georgia, with his mother and his sister, Helen.*

Once when we were all three eating watermelon on the back porch, Helen and I were having fun spitting watermelon seeds over the railing. We grew inspired by the many watermelon seeds. We began planting them all over the backyard—digging holes with kitchen spoons, pouring in watermelon seeds, and then covering up the holes—thinking that in the fecund earth of Savannah watermelon vines would sprout effortlessly and that by the end of the summer there would be huge watermelons all over the backyard.

We waited and waited. But at the end of the summer, to our great disappointment, no watermelons had sprouted.

The next summer we decided to set up one of those collapsible swimming pools. So we got one and set it up in the backyard—this huge drum of corrugated iron that came up to here on me [gestures to throat] with a bottom of swimming pool blue rubber. Then we turned on the hose and began filling up the pool—which took hours. We watched in fascination as the water rose. Filling the pool was probably the most satisfying thing about it. Before it was half full, we jumped in and let the water rise around us.

But after a few days we barely used the swimming pool. We were on the go in the car so much—driving to Hilton Head, or to the beach at Tybee, or to swim in the Ogeechee River, or in the river at Bluffton. The water in the swimming pool grew opaque—ink black. Leaves and branches floated across its surface—and God knows what lurked in its depths. It was more forbidding than any swamp. No one in their right mind would have gotten into it. It remained brimful as well—replenished by the summer's many rains.

All through that summer the pool exercised a strange fascination over the backyard. It was tall and mysterious. The rain went across it and its mystery was stirred and we wondered at its depths. We would gaze at the black surface of the pool and imagine strange monsters lurking there—ghastly things—corpses.

Finally one day we destroyed the pool. We attacked it gleefully, bashing down its sides and watching in delight as the black water poured out in all directions. We kept waiting for monsters to be revealed. I think we were all three convinced there was a human corpse hidden in those waters. But there was nothing in the pool. It was empty.

But at the bottom of the pool a mystery entirely unexpected awaited us. The rubber bottom of the pool, now black with sludge, rose up in strange humps everywhere. There were things underneath the pool's bottom. What could these things be? The thought was horrifying.

We all three grabbed the sides of the pool and began heaving it up—peeling it from the ground. What we saw was more horrifying than anything we could ever have imagined. There were watermelons everywhere—huge watermelons. But they were white —absolutely white—albino watermelons. The watermelons we had planted had been growing there, trapped under the swimming pool—trapped growing blindly in the dark. Their whiteness was as horrible as the horror of their fate. We could not bring ourselves to touch them. And the thought of slicing one open to see what it was like inside was unimaginable. How we got rid of them I don't remember. Such was the fate of the albino watermelons.

The Story

SARAH WOLBACH

When my mother crashed the car I was five.
       The rest of the story: *You went through the windshield.*
I wonder.

       Did my face fracture glass?
           Was I shattered like sand?
               Was I shot through the glass like a dream
child flying?

Probably
I banged my head
and crumpled on the floor.

                          under a thousand blinding suns
                          white-masked monsters sewed me up
                          taught me to scream

I'm still going through the windshield like the arrow in Zeno's paradox
infinitely dividing the space but never reaching the target or the ground
(or the story)
or now.

Bullet Therapy

GIL FAGIANI

If I hadn't shot my brother, we wouldn't have a relationship now. My older brother, Teddy, is a gorilla, and when we were kids, he liked to smack around me and my younger brother, Tommy. My father was in a mental institution in Florida and Mom worked six days a week, so it wasn't like there was a lot of adult supervision. Teddy, who was the biggest and strongest, could never admit that he was wrong, and if you argued with him, sooner or later he would start using his hands. My brother Tommy broke a bottle over his head a couple of times and this calmed him down. In fact, after he did this, Teddy acted like nothing happened, like everything was just hunky-dory, while we were climbing the walls. I couldn't take it anymore, and the next time he looked like he was going to lose it, I went into my room and came out with my .22. When Teddy saw it, he rushed me. I guess he thought he could grab the gun or intimidate me into not pulling the trigger. But I shot him in the arm. Later, we told the doctors in the ER that Teddy had been winged in the park by some gangbangers. Teddy is still a gorilla, but he doesn't dare lay a hand on me. If I hadn't shot him, I would have had to cut him loose and never see him again.

The Dusk-Tinged Rooftop Television Antennas of My Childhood

SEAN THOMAS DOUGHERTY

Your eyes turned into a city & the city
turned into a downhill block
where I rode a basketball in my backpack
on a yellow bike beneath dusk-tinged
television antenna'd skies
& in my mind was only the scent
of summer & sweat & the asphalt court
with faded lines where Andre & Little Alex
& T were waiting to play all day sinking
jump shots into the chain-less rim
& even the rain falling slowly & warm
is the space between your legs
is what I was wading through & wanting
to drown in even then I was heading
towards you a city where I would live
these decades & tumble & when I kiss
you I am there back there riding my bicycle
long before Garry was dead,
long before the assault charges
and the redemption, before job
after stupid job & decades
before you became ill,

before miscarriages & disease,
& how for many years I told you
you looked so much like Audrey Hepburn
in *Roman Holiday* & I was Gregory Peck,
driving you away from the paparazzi—
these fictions we create to survive,
you my city of voluminous heights
& alleys of secrets, & the light
of grace falling across your face,
even here in a basement apartment,
in a city along a big dirty lake,
& the other city inside you,
& the sky over that city,
the one I am flying through as you open
your mouth, teaching me the shape
of my own city, the borders
& boundaries & how they bleed.
& the dialects & music, the choruses
we claim, the benches where we will
sit when we are old, & never leaving,
until I realize you will be dead,
long ravished by this thing
inside you no one can name,
now even your teeth are gone, the wounds
on your feet, your thinning hair, & this necropolis
we wander, what adjectives to cull, no subject
to seam along the rim of the far boulevards & banks,
but then I look up to find the sky, the sky inside you,
the sky inside me & your sentence
is the air that never ebbs, & like a city
seen from on high I see that you & I

have always been part of this web,
the way our hands meld
& merge & that street I traveled on
long before I met you vanishes,
& the future's opaque clouds clear,
& here we are holding one other,
on a basement couch, building
with each breath the parapets
& obelisks of love's metropolis
against the constant arrival

Too Sexy

MATTILDA BERNSTEIN SYCAMORE

Avery calls me up and says Alexa, I figured it out.

You figured what out?

I figured it out, Alexa, I figured it out I figured it out I figured it out!

Honey, you are coked out of your mind.

Alexa, who isn't? But listen up, I know you're always talking about how everyone in Boston is totally apathetic and I'm like the worst example I mean I don't even have a political bone in my body—I know I was a PoliSci major for like ten minutes, but I didn't even know what was going on I thought PoliSci was science. Alexa, there are so many problems, so many problems and I know you know that I know I know I know, Alexa. But what was I saying, what was I saying? Oh—I still don't fucking know what's going on, but I thought of something we can do together—oh, maybe I shouldn't say it on the phone. Alexa, it's true, I have to wait at the haunted house for a few deliveries, but I'll tell you my idea later, when I see you. I think you'll like it. I think you'll really like it. Really really. I'm sure. I'm really sure. Okay?

Later, Avery and I are at Bertucci's and she looks around to make sure no one's paying attention and then says listen, Alexa, listen: Remember when we went to Star Market last night to get contact lens solution? Yes, last night, that was last night! Okay, so I was looking around at everyone looking at you. Everyone. And no one, no one at all, no one was looking at me. You see what I mean?

Not exactly.

Alexa, don't play coy with me, coy decoy, you're the one who likes to call it bargain shopping. No one was looking at me, get it?

Oh, okay, yes, yes, I get it. Bargain shopping realness. I knew it, Alexa, I knew it! And, you're right about something else—I should smoke more pot, I didn't realize I could be so hungry, even though there isn't any fucking cheese in this pizza it's yummy, almost as yummy as you and here's my example, it's cold out, right? Really fucking freezing-your-ass-off cold. So what do people need, people outside? People stuck the fuck outside in this fucking freezing cold. Sleeping bags, right?

Usually I'm so focused on my own bargain shopping, studying everyone's reactions while I yawn and pretend to be oh-so-relaxed. Wait, did I tell you how relaxed I am? Honey, I could almost fall asleep right here. Everyone looks at my hair, but then there's the moment when they look away and that's when I liberate those $70 vitamins.

But it's so much easier when all I have to do is take in the attention, bask in it, glow. Whenever someone glances in Avery's direction, I ask some idiotic question or act like I'm about to slip a hula hoop into my purse and boom, all eyes are on me. Eight sleeping bags in one afternoon—we can't help adding up the prices on the labels, just to see. Okay, goodbye evidence. Hello homeless shelter. Let's just drop these off outside.

Remember *Drugstore Cowboy*? I think that's the only movie I've seen three times. Except for *The Unbelievable Truth*, where in the beginning two girls are lying in the grass looking up at the sky while talking to one another and that's kind of how I feel in the car with Avery, doing another bump of coke and this is our movie, shot from inside a cream-colored Mercedes. It's probably not called cream. Avery, what do they call this color?

Breathe deep and let your head roll back and then step outside like you don't even notice the camera's on you, yes, you. Every store has plenty of mirrors, even if they're selling sporting goods in Allston, Cambridge, Brookline—and everybody knows mirrors are for runway. High-level undercover stunway. Honey, what is all this gear for? Bug smearer. Rain fearer. Forty-degrees-below-zero dream gear hair smear bug fear right here, turn.

Think about waving, waving for the cameras. Especially when they're playing "Highway to Hell." Think, but don't look. Yawn again. Turn. Avery's out the door. Pose. Let the lights blend into your eyes. Walk.

Another bump? Of course, darling, of course—you always know how to provide.

The good thing about the coke cure is that it helps with my cough. No, seriously. Just a little bump and I'm fine. Another bump and I'm even better. A third bump and the cough is practically gone. Or, if not, what a perfect distraction—AIDS alert in aisle four. And then: runway runaway.

Avery, you're right, you're right, this is fun. Fun for the whole family. Whose family?

"Brighter Days," girl—brighter days brighter days brighter days! But what am I making for dinner yes dinner, do you want to come over, no, probably not a good idea, I mean not right at this moment.

Why not at this moment—you don't want Sugar Daddy to see you with your bitchy boyfriend?

I don't want him to see me with my bitchy boyfriend when we're both coked out of our minds.

I am not coked out of my mind, I'm coked into my mind.

Girl, that's brilliant, but wait, today's the day we get our test results.

Here we are on Boylston, opening the door in the wind tunnel and then checking in at the front desk where the receptionist gives us that fake smile and then waves us into the waiting room dungeon. Clinics are so depressing. It's like they're just waiting for you to die. Why can't they at least play good music, something with a beat, maybe a DJ and a dance floor, they could easily fit a disco ball over there in that corner by the dusty plastic flowers.

What about real flowers—even something cheap, carnations, what about carnations? What about art on the walls, I'm sure there are plenty of rich bitches who would be glad to donate art, or if not then give me a couple of twenties and I'll go to the thrift store to find some wacky glamour. Or at least paint the walls bright colors instead of this atrocious faded gray-and-tan wallpaper—we're here to take care of ourselves, not to fade into nothingness. What about velvet sofas and herbal tea and steamed vegetables and brown rice and maybe something to read besides pamphlets about STDs?

What if the clinic was like a café where you could hang out and gossip and cruise or even read a good book, there could be a library or free massage or acupuncture or hugs, right, what about hugs? Instead of hugs we just get sterile beige carpet and hand-me-down office chairs and a few boring ads for safe sex. What about makeup lessons or a reading group? If no one wants to read, we could read Kevyn Aucoin and practice all the tricks, I wouldn't mind practicing makeup tricks with a bunch of queens at the STD clinic. What about a DJ-ing workshop, I would love a DJ-ing workshop. Art supplies—what about art supplies?

They call my number and Avery's still holding my hand and I'm thinking about colored pencils and crayons and magic markers and oil pastels. Or, what about making collages? The clinic would be such a great place to make a collage—it wouldn't even cost anything. Everyone could just bring in their old magazines and cut and paste and get to know one another. It would be fun.

Avery's squeezing my hand tighter, I can't believe she's twenty-three but she's never been tested before. They call my number again and then I'm in another sterile room, this one feels like they sucked out all the air and some blonde woman in a powder blue cardigan with pearly buttons asks me what I would do if I tested positive.

I have nothing against powder blue cardigans, and especially not powder blue cardigans with pearly buttons, I mean I have a lavender one just like that. But that strand of pearls around her neck. Real pearls.

Those pearls, I want to say. What are you trying to say with those pearls?

How would you react if you tested positive, she asks me again.

Honey, I'm thinking, I would jump off a bridge. Can you take me to the highest bridge? I need a ride. You don't drive? Then at least give me directions.

I want to say that I would go out and do so many drugs that I wouldn't even know my name. But instead I just say I don't know.

She asks me about my risks. I don't ask about hers. Is she going to give me my results?

After she suggests condoms for oral sex—yeah, already tried that—she finally looks down at the piece of paper and says: You tested negative for HIV. Thank you for coming in today. Do you have any questions for me?

Back in the waiting room, now I'm nervous while waiting for Avery, until he comes out with a smile. I can't believe how hot it is in here, I'm totally covered in sweat.

We get to Avery's and she pours a bunch of coke on the mirror without even taking off her coat, snorts way too much, and then shakes her head back and forth and starts jumping up and down. She hands me the mirror, says let me hold you while you do it—come on, come on, hurry up, catch up with me—and then I'll bend you over and fuck you over the sink.

I thought you never wanted to have sex again.

That was before.

I wake up the next day singing some punk love song that I don't even know the words to, and then Avery's singing along and I say yes, that song, who sings it?

I'm just imitating you.

The way it all blends together, one day and then the next. One store and then the next. One line and then the next. The day we wheel a whole shopping cart full of canned food out of Star Market, hello food drive. And then the next Star Market. And the next. Honey, who's the star now?

That feeling in my head, where am I, that feeling when I'm sitting with Ned and he's speaking and I'm trying to pay attention—oh, right, another cocktail, thank you. That feeling in my head, so warm and cool at the same time, blending these pills and powders and potions and yes, that feeling in my head, hold me.

The way my eyes can be blue but really that's white and blue and a circle of green, sparkly brown spots on the left I never realized brown could sparkle is it really purple in disguise like the way the white of the eyes is the part that shines the most and you never realize that from far away. Or the way skin is really all these little holes, some dry and some greasy even after the apricot facial scrub and oil-free moisturizer it's never just smooth except from far away and I guess that's why so many people wear so much makeup. But even the bags under my eyes can become pretty when I stare long enough and let everything blur. Look, look how my lower lip is bigger and puffier and redder than the upper lip.

And now, our special guests for the evening: Teeth—that's just the way you are—teeth. We think of you as white, but that's only compared to night. So much closer to yellow, hello—unless you've been bleached. Bleached, leeched and impeached.

No, don't impeach my teeth—I swear they didn't mean to lie when they said they were light-bright spite fright mighty fighty tighty-whitey, I swear.

Really, stop looking for stains, okay? Stop pulling back skin to disguise structure. Focus on the way the water pours over your hands in little tiny waterfalls, all this hot water for my hands, oatmeal soap a massage until I'm ready to take out my contacts, right, I'm taking out my contacts. And then, time for magical Marinol, oh yes.

Avery rings the bell and when I get to the door in my robe he's standing there with sunflowers, what a great way to start the day. Then she reaches down and picks up a boombox, where'd you get that boombox?

I'm bringing back the '80s.

Oh, no, please, not the '80s. Anything but the '80s. Even the '70s, I mean you know how much I hate disco but anything's better than Michael Jackson. Thank you for the flowers, they're beautiful.

Okay, the early-90s. You're beautiful.

Avery wants to watch the sunset, and when we get to the Esplanade it's almost warm out—I mean it's freezing, but at least there's no wind. Look at those pink clouds over there, someone's finally lighting the Citgo sign on fire. Avery puts the boombox down and says wait, wait until you hear this. And she presses play.

No way. The beat starts and I can't help it, I'm flinging myself into the air and around, falling to the ground and rolling in the frozen grass towards water and then jumping across the paved part and back again for more space, give her, give her what, give her the river, deliver, shiver, my liver, and Avery's clapping and I'm throwing my arms everywhere, hands flying up and back, head in every direction, yes there are a few tourists and joggers who look scared, yes I do the big kick in the air as high as possible and I land with one leg straight out and the other crossed underneath like I'm just sitting there so calmly. Avery comes over to fan me with her hand, and that's when I jump up and twist around her, is this another mix, how many mixes are there?

And there's that beat like one of those movie songs—girl, where the hell did you get "I'm Too Sexy" anyway? Okay, okay, here I go, running down the Esplanade and Avery's cackling and I start to twirl around and around and around until I'm dizzy enough that doing the falling-over runway really is falling, bending side to side and taking the tight rope into fight rope, light rope, blight rope, smash the glass and jump-up-and-down delight rope and Avery runs in front of me and I stop, turn, put my hand on her face and then we turn around together, I'm holding onto her back like I could hold on forever but then I push her aside and she laughs and what is this mix, I don't remember this mix and now I'm leaning back against Avery like a prop or a wall or treasure or the end of the line or sustenance.

Feelings
(for Eileen Myles)

EMMA WOOTTON

they always warned us against
using the lyrical i in poems, of

making them too personal. but
how can i explain morning, the

perfect chance of waking to you, if
nobody is interested in my

voice. after all—what does it matter
what you say about yourself, which

name you choose or how you
write the quiet intensity of simply

breathing in an age where all
we care about is following the

money & the trends that will
pay us & the products we can

buy when the trends that we have
followed have given us the money

that they promised. spread the
word before someone else spreads

theirs & you are even harder to
believe.

we had better be careful, writing
about our feelings so unashamedly.

we have tried inventing new ways &
new words & tried to make everything

new again, we have dallied with abstraction &
revelled in some pretty explicit depictions, we

have defined who we are only to
hurriedly erase them, these

definitions that are unmoving &
certain to prevent us from expressing in

the accepted, intellectual way. we have
read all the theories on the current

curriculum & aced papers on Marvell &
Derrida & Dickinson but still the

urge to write about our feelings in
only the way a poem can make us feel

is niggling away between worn leather
casings & refusing to be anything other

than this. i do it all for love, which seems
ridiculous, knowing as i do that nothing

lasts forever, but if i could ever really
bruise you with my feelings, i'd

stand a chance of leaving something
more viable behind than a string of

phrases on a page that strangers will
read & only recognise fleeting moments

of in their own lives when they watch
you walk in or out of the door for

the very last time.

Where's Guadalupe

CASSANDRA DALLETT

Flaco was beautiful
and sometimes I wonder if he made it out alive.
Last time I saw him he was a Marine.
Quiet smooth Flaco wearing Marine sweatpants like a white boy.
I can't imagine him in the foreign violence of that life.
I wonder does he know his whole neighborhood
has gone as white as a field of dandelion gone to seed.
And where did all his brothers go.
A slick creased crew of them crowding his Mother's stoop on Duboce.
Did he survive the wars
like he survived that suicide attempt in my bathroom,
that half- hearted help, a plastic Bic and a Band-Aid.
Was it Sandra Osario's rejection or some other poison
he carried in him when he joined us that night.
A circle on the floor of our furniture-less apartment,
a bottle or two passed, maybe it was still the year of 7&7,
I don't think I'd graduated to gin and grapefruit yet.
It was my first apartment.
I kept it immaculate. Everything had its place.
Jobless days I swept the wood floors
and watched the fog roll over Twin Peaks.
My old neighborhood is lily white now too,
a rent increased by thousands.
Tech buses idle the intersections these days,

but when I went into the bathroom
I saw the razor out of place and the Band Aids.
I called in the other guys to conference, we were drunk goofy drunk,
and I guess Brad was gonna make it with Sandra that time,
leaving Josh greasy in his third wheel army jacket,
and me with Flaco who rubbed into my back all night,
trying to get my pants down and put it inside me.
I played dumb and stiff, begged Josh to stay, to keep talking,
while Flaco waved his hands at him from behind me, to get lost.
I wanted to tell Flaco to stop,
well really I wanted to ask why he'd cut himself.
I wanted to tell him he was still as fine as he had been back in the day
when I stole his number from the principal's office.
When even the black girls were like that's Gaudalupe's fine ass,
so shy and mysterious, the sheen of Tres Flores, the shine on his shoes.
Was there always something so sad in eyes.
The eyes I refused to look at
as I gave him my back and wordlessly
let him dry hump me till day's light.

An Absurd Madness

RICHARD FEIN

Horn & Hardart long extinct, forgotten by generations x, y, and z.
An old fashion cafeteria, especially for cabbies at the end of their shifts.
Tables for a random shuffle of eight hungry strangers,
and at mine there were two very strange strangers, that cabbie and me.
That cabbie took his seat opposite me and began his culinary catechism.
A forkful of meatloaf, a forkful of mashed potato, a forkful of peas, a sip of lemonade.
A forkful of meatloaf, a forkful of mashed potato, a forkful of peas, a sip of lemonade.
A forkful of meatloaf, a forkful of mashed potato, a forkful of peas, a sip of lemonade.
An ad nauseam pitiless predictable parade of dining plate portions.
Not peas then meatloaf. Not peas before potato. Not meatloaf and skip the peas for now.
And not a sip of lemonade somewhere or anywhere in between.
Meatloaf and lemonade, lemonade and meatloaf were the perpetual brackets of his repast.
A forkful of meatloaf, a forkful of mashed potato, a forkful of peas, a sip of lemonade.
A forkful of meatloaf, a forkful of mashed potato, a forkful of peas, a sip of lemonade.
Twenty-four permutations were possible but the probability reduced to a maddening one,
a forkful of meatloaf, a forkful of mashed potato, a forkful of peas, a sip of lemonade.
There was a very strange person at that automat table—me.
The cabbie was breaking no laws. Why should I have cared? Was none of my business.
Besides, my shirt was stained with enough gravy to cover his meatloaf.
But his obsessive behavior made me think of murder, murder, murder, murder, murder.
But that was years ago. I'm a much more sedated diner now.
I feel so laid back, so laid back, oh so laid back.
And how easy to write this digital poem, highlight, cut, and paste on the screen.
No more pens running out of ink. No more writer's cramp fingers to forever record,

A forkful of meatloaf, a forkful of mashed potato, a forkful of peas, a sip of lemonade.
Just a click, click, click and this repetitive verse is wholly redundantly entirely done.
Oh I feel so laid back. I'm so much calmer now.
Except, here at Starbucks there is this one sitting at the next table.
I'm watching him and keeping meticulous account of his peculiar culinary proclivities.
A bite of sandwich, a piece of cake, a sip of coffee, a pat of napkin on the lips.

Mediocrity Is the New Black

PENNY ARCADE

Based on a monologue for a 2014 two-week, sold-out performance at Joe's Pub, New York City.

When I was eight years old, my mother took my sister, two brothers, and me to see Disney's *Snow White and the Seven Dwarves*. It was the first movie I saw on a big screen. The Strand was ornate, rococo, and plush. Coming from the afternoon sun into the dark, sensuous interior— all red velvet and dark mystery—was an intoxicating experience. I had read the book and, although I sensed it was somehow wrong, I wasn't drawn to Snow White one bit. Instead I was entranced by the Evil Queen who seemed to spend as much time looking at herself in mirrors as I did, asking "Who is the fairest of them all?" Seeing Snow White on the big screen dispelled any doubts I had about who of the two were more interesting. I was repelled by the demure, overly nice Snow White and how she dressed: all blue and red and flouncy with that awful high white collar.

The Evil Queen though was so chic. I loved her look. That tight black hood (Azzedine Alaia!) peaked in front (Mary McFadden!), the red, red lipstick (Diana Vreeland!) And then the Evil Queen knocking Snow White out with a poison apple. Yes! That Snow White was such a bore. All that goodie-goodie shit. A poison apple put Snow White into a deathlike sleep. Deep in the forest she lay in her glass coffin, surrounded and worshipped by a crowd of men. Just like Tilda Swinton in her glass box at MOMA.

From antiquity, the apple has symbolized the fruit of knowledge. Adam and Eve ate from the apple tree and they knew sin (or at least that's what the Bible says...) Back in 1921, apples were the slang for the big money prizes at the many racetracks surrounding New York City. Jockeys, trainers, and breeders arrived dreaming about this big money. The *New York Morning Telegraph* sportswriter, Jack FitzGerald, dubbed New York "The

Big Apple," writing "There's only one Big Apple. That's New York." And it has stuck as a nickname ever since.

Personally I always thought "The Big Apple" referred to the aforementioned knowledge of good and evil and therefore New York City was Sin City. I don't know about you, but most people I know came to New York to sin. New York City was the one place in America where sin was reliably available. In the '70s Mayor Lindsey branded New York "Fun City," and everyone knows sin is fun. Now New York City lies in a coma while herds of goody-goody Snow Whites and frat boy elves roam the city streets and New York has gone from the city that never sleeps to the city that can't wake up.

People used to come to New York to pursue freedom, culture, sex, glamour, decadence, drugs, art, poetry, and music. Now they come to walk past Magnolia Bakery, the location where *Sex and the City* spawned a cupcake obsession. The Big Apple to the Big Cupcake? How did that happen? The image of Sarah Jessica Parker smooshing a cupcake into her face will forever be the image of the suburban conquest of New York City. The final crumb in the coffin. Do you know about this? There are walking tours and bus tours to view the spot where Carrie porned that cupcake. There are endless articles about downtown NY now being *livable*, *desirable*. West 4th Street is Lourdes to these cupcake pilgrims who line up outside to worship at the spot where their greatest role model reified and consumed New York City as a pretty, sugary treat. An accessory that could also be consumed and, if need be, easily purged. The gutters around the Magnolia Bakery run brown with the puke of bulimics and in the time since that episode aired, West 4th has gone from being a bohemian holdout to a street of impossibly high-priced designer shops.

Seriously, there are now a hundred cupcake shops in a twenty square block radius of my apartment. People stagger from one cupcake shop to another. A de-cultured zombie horde leaving a trail of cupcake crumbs across the city. These people want a cupcake the way I want a cigarette, the way I want a joint. Cupcakes are the latest narcotic of the infantilized masses. These people are addicted to the idea of cupcakes like they are addicted to social media, prescription drugs, internet porn, and computer games. It is an epidemic. So many people suffering from OCD. Obsessive cupcake disorder!

There is a vast larvae of people between the ages of eighteen and forty who have been sold New York City as a social destination. Corralled through advertising and television shows like *Sex and the City* and *Girls* (and before that *Friends*, *Seinfeld*, and *Felicity*), they form a culture that merges perpetual Spring Break and The Singles Scene. These people will spend an average of two to seven years in NYC in a consumer orgy marketed to them as a kind of capitalist identity quest until finally one day—having sowed their "non-conventional" wild oats—they pull up their stakes and head back, in a final Craigslist sale and potlatch, to take their place in assembly line conformity. Back home and forever the envy of their peers at the PTA and Little League barbeques. The streets of NYC are mobbed by what some of us refer to as "The Princess Plague."

These hordes of snow-white girls roam New York walking four abreast like their role models from the *Sex and the City* opening credits. They wobble on high heels, lurch drunk in skimpy outfits, hog the city sidewalks like the mall rats they once were. They're twenty-five-years old but they dress like fifty-year-old cougars, wearing $7,000 worth of clothes if you count their handbags and shoes. Crowds of drunken former frat boys, hooting and howling in the streets, follow them. The girls want to get married and the boys want to get laid. Yes, cupcakes are for girls and the boys who want to fuck them. Those girls want a cupcake. Those boys want a blowjob. Maybe if they cover their dick in frosting, they'll get one...

People who hate history, culture and authenticity love cupcakes, because cupcakes are retro, vintage, and nostalgic. These Stepford Hipsters love cupcakes because cupcakes don't ask hard questions. Cupcakes understand! Cupcakes are for kids, for narcissists, sociopaths and psychopaths—who are what children are until they are socialized.

Cupcakes are the perfect totem for people who have never left their suburban childhoods, even as they swill mojitos, artisanal beers, ramen and sushi in the designated shopping corridors that now define New York City. The cupcake hovers over their psyche. It's their blankey. The perfect childhood memory that helps them maintain their infantilized self in the face of their sophisticated posture.

The cupcake represents conformity, selfishness, and self-absorption. The body of the cupcake is drab and, after the first bite, boring. It doesn't even have a filling. Unlike the original trashy Hostess Cupcake of yore that had a slab of sugared fat at its heart, beneath the frosting each cupcake is the same and ultimately cupcakes are empty.

Cupcakes are perfect for people who can only handle bite-sized information, which fits in perfectly with their communication methods, which never reach out, and only boomerang back to them, reflected, like selfies in their tweets, texts, and Instagrams or Facebook posts. Since it's hard to share a cupcake, cupcakes help keep their fragile sense of individuality whole. They can telegraph their personality style through their choice of cupcake: Sexy? *Red Velvet*. Impulsive? *Salted Caramel*. Spunky? *Lemon Ginger*. Cheerful? *Blueberry*.

Though the cupcake seems innocent, it is malevolent. Cupcakes perfectly represent what Hannah Arendt called the banality of evil. Cupcakes give these fragile people who are being programmed to move to New York a false sense of security, that everything will be safe, predictable, nice and mall-like, just like the gated communities across America that spawned them.

The cupcake is a tool of gentrification so it is a tool of oppression. The gentrification of a poor neighborhood always starts with a café and always ends with a cupcake shop. Cupcakes are the essence of passive-aggression, just like the middle class manners that have invaded New York through these mallster zombies. Manners that hide their entitlement in the face of the marginalization of poor people, the displacement of the working poor and underclass by gentrification, in a form of saccharine niceness that doesn't measure the damage they inflict by their presence.

Colonization has never tasted so sweet.

Make a 5–Year Plan

JOSH STEINBAUER

☐ Move to Europe
Get a book on calligraphy and fonts
Work a stand on a bridge, engraving couples' names into locks
Wed the shopkeep who sells the only bolt cutters in town
Live off the river's endless coming and going

☐ Find a cottage near a lighthouse in Maine
Buy a rowboat, some oil paints
Fill local diners with foggy impressions of departed beacons
Spend bachelor nights doodling a pornographic comic book
(an erotic courtroom duo: *FudgePuree and Sexecutioner*)

☐ Lease a loft above a bookstore
Put the remaining 9,500 hours into a guitar
Tour Japan in a band called *Fights About Farts*
Meet some Yoko, become a dad, tour the family band
Spoiler Alert (concept band: kids' songs that ruin endings)

☐ Go back to school (repetition is the basis for meaning)
Bury cans of beer like seeds of happiness (again)
Dissertate on sea mammal linguistics: *"Echolocution"*
Return their spliced trills and chirps as poems and radio plays
Sail autumn migrations as their tinny parrot (or their burning bush)

☐   Take out a loan to start an app company
Marry a Russian (good programmers!)
Develop *"Breadcrumbs"* app—continual cloud's eye selfies
Release 2.0 w/ *Boomerang* feature—right back here in 5 years
Happier, having unfolded like old maps we no longer need

The Engineer

MATT PASCA

The engineer's early years are marked by his abuse
of immediate family:

little brother in the dryer, 20 minute knit cycle,
he squats in front of the circular window, entranced.

He fits a can of Cheez Whiz in the Thanksgiving
turkey his mother is baking in the oven, having read

its disclaimer: *Caution: flammable if exposed*
to sudden changes in temperature. Late afternoon,

the engineer's mother's eyebrows and hair are singed
when she opens the oven door. The engineer feels triumphant.

At college, the engineer knocks on Jennifer's door, recites
the lyrics to *Part of Your World* in a monotone, nearly digital

voice, because the un-mermaid-like engineer cannot carry
a tune. A white towel drapes his slender, brown neck

because he sweats continually. He is reticent to shake
others' hands for this reason. Jennifer invites him in.

He says her ass reminds him of binary code, is confused
when she asks him to leave. He sings *Kiss the Girl*

in a stilted Caribbean accent then walks home, dribbling
an imaginary basketball to *Under the Sea*.

The engineer's father, out to dinner with his wife
for their 25th wedding anniversary, tells the waitress:

Your chest is symmetrical. He is a statistician and
explains that her breasts are precisely aligned,

mathematically perfect. The engineer's mother
swears off year 26, curses arranged marriage.

Later, the engineer works for the government by day,
watches *Temptation Island* by night. He notices

in the credits the *island nation of Costa Rica* is thanked
for its permission to film. The engineer is apoplectic,

writes the network about how disillusioned he's become
because of their mistake. *Costa Rica is not an island*,

the engineer writes. *You could have avoided insulting
my intelligence by calling it "Temptation Isthmus"*.

The network sends him two free tickets to Universal Studios.
The engineer is still mad.

Weeks later, the engineer writes another letter, to *People
Magazine*, after a headline that called Ben Affleck

tall, dark and handsome. The engineer, whose family
is from Bangladesh, asks *People* if they think Ben Affleck's mom

ever told him to smile both ways before crossing the street at night.
People sends him a free subscription. The engineer is still mad.

One night, the engineer decides to play with the garage
circuit breakers at 3 a.m. His cousin, a writer, is in town, working

on a manuscript upstairs. The house goes dark. Two chapters
are lost. The engineer does not apologize to his cousin.

The engineer has yet to apologize.
For anything.

Eponymous

KARL ROULSTON

Leave them a part of your parcels, the lion's share in shards, then hunt and peck for grails in graves and guide the tide with tugs. Spray the surf with sand. The spaces you spot on the banks of the flood are farms for a thought crop. Plots for your floor plans. The bliss that you feel in the felt of your hat is the band that you hear in your dreams. Pitch, yaw and roll. Fold, spindle and mitigate. The years that you spent spilling beans in the bistro return on the bikes that you left in the barrens to rest in the sun and rust in the rain, so bolster your bluster and burnish the brogue you brandish. Spread it like brutish butter. Say, "They call me Rudy Reese but I'm known as Randy Rex. I've run a million miles and I'm here to read your meters. West of the blessed fields and east of the humble hills, the last of the royal wrens have ripped the rounder's writs and I'm here to rub your rags. I'm here to wax your Rolls." All they can do is flip you the bird, so hand 'em the bill and beat it. With press kit and cat case. Ascot and inkwell. Know it in the rustic sack you stuffed with busted buckles. Know in your bones your burden's a bourbon you hold in abeyance, so let it sink in the sea of souls. Let it simmer in the bouillabaisse. Rise with the mist and mix with the clouds and drop with the drizzle. Land on the land. Seep to the roots and flow to the branches. Leave with the leaves and float on the wind. Say, "This is the glue that holds all the blue notes." Say, "This is the crack in the glass of glissando and these are the whirling words." Lord, lord, lord.

Primitive Tools

LYNETTE REINI-GRANDELL

A stone and a stone and a stone am I,
without fur, not the strongest.
I am tracking what is missing inside,
hungry for the hard grain that has not moved.

What does it take to wake the icebound earth?

This slow stillness keeps forgetting to breathe;
the seed may never be born.
But I have learned to forge iron.
I have learned to make a knife.

Leave a Little Room for Jesus, He Said

REBECCA AUDRA SMITH

I was kissing you, necking on
the Canal Street love boat. We edged up
in our seats and made some space for Jesus
to sit down. Tight squeeze, my kneecaps
knocking yours, my tongue still in your
mouth, not much room for his words.
Still, he started to preach. Jesus
is the man to call when you want
two women to pull apart. Jesus
is the place to go when you want
us to rearrange our bodies till we
sit decorous as flowers in a vase.
Jesus is the man to speak to
when you want to unlink our hands.
I haven't space enough on this paper
to tell him that I will kiss you
wherever I fucking want to.

CONTRIBUTORS

ALEPH ALTMAN-MILLS is an autistic writer who collects acorns and likes to buy books other people have already written on. She has been published in *The Legendary* and lives in Massachusetts.

PENNY ARCADE is a performance artist, writer, poet, and experimental theatre maker known for her magnetic stage presence, her take no prisoners wit, and her content-rich plays and one-liners. She is the author of ten scripted performance plays and hundreds of performance art pieces. Her decades-long focus on the creation of community and inclusion as the goals of performance, and her efforts to use performance as a transformative act, mark Penny Arcade as a true original in American theatre and performance.

Born and raised in Flatbush, Brooklyn, **AMBER ATIYA** is the author of the chapbook *the fierce bums of doo-wop* (Argos Books, 2014). Her work has appeared in *Boston Review*, *Nepantla: A Journal Dedicated to Queer Poets of Color*, *Bone Bouquet*, *Black Renaissance Noire*, and elsewhere. A 2012 Poets House Fellow, Amber is a proud member of a women's writing group that will be celebrating thirteen years this spring.

TONI LA REE BENNETT is a poet, photographer, editor, and perennial student. She received a PhD in English from the University of Washington and continues to study there. Her writing and photography have appeared in publications including *Journal of Poetry Therapy*, *California Quarterly*, *Hawai'i Pacific Review*, *Puerto del Sol*, *Glassworks*, and the Seattle *Poetry on Buses* project. She edited the online journal *Branches* and operated her own publishing house, Uccelli Press. Toni shares her Seattle space with a flock of feisty finches.

JENNIFER BLOWDRYER is a writer by nature, although the genres change by year and inspiration. She has written a novel, a memoir, a dictionary, and an advice book. She was a co-founder of seminal punk bands The Blowdryers, The White Trash Debutantes, and currently fronts The Jennifer Blowdryer Band. In her teens, she created Smut Fests when sex work was taboo. Her most recent chapbook is *Blowsy* (Personality Press, 2014).

MEAGAN BROTHERS is the author of two novels for young adults, *Debbie Harry Sings in French* and *Supergirl Mixtapes*. Her latest YA novel is W*eird Girl and What's-His-Name* (Three Rooms Press, 2015). Her poetry has appeared, or is forthcoming, in *Night Bomb Review*, *The Wormwood Press*, and *Grabbing the Apple*.

KEAH BROWN is a reader not a fighter. A lover and a writer. She has a BA in Journalism from The State University of New York at Fredonia, and her work can be found in *Cactus Heart Literary Magazine*, *Vine Leaves Literary Journal*, *Saturday Night Reader*, and *The Rain, Party, & Disaster Society*. She loves TV and tweets @Keah_Maria about cheesecake and how she should be writing.

RYAN BUYNAK is a butthead who hates writing bios, but he is thankful for alliteration. He is probably somewhere right now listening to music or yelling at someone.

BILLY CANCEL has recently appeared in *Blazevox*, *Other Rooms Press*, and *Bombay Gin*. His latest collection, *Gauze Coast*, was published by Hidden House Press in 2015.

LAUREN MARIE CAPPELLO has traded in the glitter of New Orleans for homesteading in Northern California. Her work has appeared in *It's Animal but Merciful* (great weather for MEDIA), *E·ratio 20*, and *The Solitary Plover*, among others.

DOROTHY CHAN was a 2014 finalist for the Ruth Lilly and Dorothy Sargent Rosenberg Poetry Fellowship. Her work has appeared, or is forthcoming, in *Blackbird*, *Spillway*, *The Great American Poetry Show*, *Plume*, and *The Writing Disorder*.

With extensive feature readings throughout New York City and environs, **JAY CHOLLICK** has frequently been interviewed on television and radio. He is the author of three books: *American Vesuvius* (The Alabama State Poetry Society), *Jay Chollick's Colors* (Exot Books), and *FiveO: The Stately Poems* (Vault Books).

DOUGLAS COLLURA is the author of *Things I Can Fit My Whole Head Into*, a finalist for the Paterson Poetry Prize. He has also released a spoken-word CD, *The Dare of the Quick World*, and is a former winner of the Missouri Review Audio/Video Competition in Poetry. Find Douglas' work in *The Alembic*, *Crack the Spine*, *Forge*, *Spillway*, *Salt Hill*, and numerous other journals.

CRAIG COTTER was born in 1960 in New York and has lived in California since 1986. New poems have appeared in *Hawai'i Review*, *Columbia Poetry Review*, *Poetry New Zealand*, *Court Green*, *Eleven Eleven*, and *Tampa Review*. His fourth book of poetry, *After Lunch with Frank O'Hara*, is available from Chelsea Station Editions.

Poet/collagist **STEVE DALACHINSKY** was born in Brooklyn after the last big war and has managed to survive lots of little wars. His book *The Final Nite* (Ugly Duckling Presse) won the PEN Oakland National Book Award. His most recent books are *Fools Gold* (Feral Press, 2014), *A Superintendent's Eyes* (Unbearable Books/Autonomedia, revised and expanded 2013), and *Flying Home*, a collaboration with German visual artist Sig Bang Schmidt (Paris Lit Up Press, 2015). Steve is a recipient of a Chevalier de l'Ordre des Artes et des Lettres.

CASSANDRA DALLETT lives in Oakland, California. She is the author of *Wet Reckless* (Manic D Press, 2014), *Bad Sandy* (Dangerous Hair Press, 2015), and several chapbooks. In addition, she has published in numerous journals such as *Slipstream*, *Chiron Review*, *Sparkle and Blink*, and *Up The River*. Cassandra was the winner of the March 2015 Literary Death Match in San Francisco.

ARIEL DAWN lives in Victoria, British Columbia. Her writing is featured, or forthcoming, in publications such as *Ambit, Black & Blue, minor literature(s), Flapperhouse, Litro*, and *Ink Sweat & Tears*. She spends her time reading Tarot and poetic prose and writing a novella.

Celebrated for her dynamic presence both onstage and on the page, **AUDREY DIMOLA** is a born and raised Queens, New York, writer, poet, performer, host, curator, and local arts crusader. The author of *Decisions We Make While We Dream* (2012) and *Traversals* (2014), Audrey aims always to stay wild and stay grateful—and there's a pretty good chance she's Peter Pan.

DANIEL DISSINGER, is the co-founder and Chief Operating Officer of Poetry Teachers NYC. He is also the founder of In Stereo Press, an online audio zine. Daniel currently teaches at SUNY College at Old Westbury, and is completing his Doctoral work at St. John's University where he is also an adjunct in the English department. Daniel's first chapbook, *tracing the shape...,* was published in 2012 by Shadow Mountain Press.

SEAN THOMAS DOUGHERTY is the author or editor of thirteen books including *All You Ask for Is Longing: Poems 1994-2014* (2014 BOA Editions), *Scything Grace* (2013 Etruscan Press), and *Sasha Sings the Laundry on the Line* (2010 BOA Editions). He works at a pool hall in Erie, Pennsylvania.

ALEX DREPPEC was born in 1968 near Frankfurt, Germany. He studied psychology and linguistics and went to Boulder, Colorado, for his PhD. He is an award-winning author with hundreds of publishing credits, both poetry and science, in German journals and anthologies. Having (re-)started writing poems in English, Alex began to submit them in 2013. His poems have since appeared in *Borderlands: Texas Poetry Review, Parody, The Interpreter's House*, and *The Journal*, among others.

GIL FAGIANI is an independent scholar, translator, essayist, short story writer, and poet. His poetry collections include *Stone Wall* (Bordighera Press, 2014) and the forthcoming *Logos* (Guernica Editions) which chronicles his experiences in a South Bronx drug program in the early 1970s. Gil co-curates the Italian American Writers' Association's reading series in New York City, and is an associate editor of *Feile-Festa: A Literary Arts Journal*.

ALEXIS RHONE FANCHER is the author of *How I Lost My Virginity To Michael Cohen and Other Heart Stab Poems* (Sybaritic Press, 2014). You can also find her work in *Rattle, H_NGM_N, Chiron Review, Fjords, Carbon Culture Review, Broad!,* and elsewhere. Her photography has been published worldwide. Alexis is poetry editor of *Cultural Weekly* and lives in Los Angeles.

RICHARD FEIN has been published in numerous national and international journals such as *Cordite, Paris/Atlantic, Canadian Dimension, Mississippi Review*, and *Constellations*. In addition, he is the author of the chapbook, *The Required Accompanying Cover Letter* (Parallel Press, University of Wisconsin-Madison).

RICH FERGUSON has shared the stage with Patti Smith, Wanda Coleman, and other esteemed poets and musicians and is a featured performer in the film *What About Me?* (with Michael Stipe, Michael Franti, Krishna Das, and others). Widely published in journals and anthologies including the *Los Angeles Times* and *Opium*, Rich is also the author of the poetry collection *8th & Agony* (Punk Hostage Press, 2012). He is a poetry editor at *The Nervous Breakdown*.

Originally from Belle Glade, Florida, ROBERT GIBBONS is a poet/performer now living in New York City. His first collection of poetry, *Close to the Tree*, was published by Three Rooms Press in 2012. Other credits include *Black Earth Institute*, *Fruita Pulp*, *Harlem World Magazine*, *Deep Water Literary,* and *Killer Whale Journal*.

ALAN GINSBERG is a spoken word artist from Baltimore City. They write primarily diary-styled pieces centered around gender, sexuality, mental illness, and combating gentrification while unavoidably benefiting from it. They hold no relation to the Beat poet or the infinitely cooler and more idol-worthy supreme court justice. They've competed at the Individual World Poetry Slam and would really like to write a poem that ends up being more sunrise then sunset.

CHRISTOPHER GREGGS is a young New York black poet. He teaches 8th grade E.L.A. in East New York, Brooklyn, has been published in the *Promethean Literary Journal*, and is the recipient of the Goodman Poetry prize from the City College of New York. He has performed as a featured poet at numerous venues across the city including The Inspired Word, Nuyorican Poets Cafe, and great weather for MEDIA's Spoken Word Sundays. Christopher lives in Harlem.

BRITT HARAWAY's stories and poetry have appeared in *South Dakota Review*, *Natural Bridge*, *New Madrid*, *Moon City Review,* and *BorderSenses*. He teaches at the University of Texas Rio Grande Valley and is the fiction editor for *RiverSedge Magazine*.

VICTORIA HATTERSLEY lives in Norwich, England, and works in publishing. Having finally started writing a year ago, after many years of meaning to but getting distracted, she is now working on her first novel while continuing to write short fiction. Victoria recently had a story published in *Unthology 6* by Unthank Books.

BOB HEMAN's prose poems have been anthologized in *The Best of the Prose Poem: An International Journal* (White Pine Press) and *An Introduction to the Prose Poem* (Firewheel Editions), and been published in *Levure littéraire*, *Skidrow Penthouse*, *Indefinite Space*, *House Organ*, and *Ambush Review*. He edits *CLWN WR*.

THOMAS HENRY's poetry is often surreal and uncomfortable and leaves you wondering what just happened. It's an expression of his continuous search to find out what is real. He's been published in various anthologies and has performed all over New York City and Long Island.

KAREN HILDEBRAND is chief content officer for the publisher of *Dance Magazine*. Her play, *The Old In and Out* (co-written with poet Madeline Artenberg), was produced Off-Off Broadway in 2013 by Three Rooms Press. You can find her poetry in such journals as *Poet Lore*, *Blue Earth Review*, *Nimrod*, *decomP magazineE*, *Maintenant*, and *Stickman Review*. In 2015, she was guest artist-in-residence at Ravens View Farm, an organic orchard in British Columbia.

LATEESHA BYNUM HINTON is a graduate of the University of North Texas and is currently a graduate student at the University of Texas at Arlington. She has four beautiful children and lives in Dallas, Texas, with her husband.

MATTHEW HUPERT is a guerilla ontologist, a raconteur, and a rhythmic rake. The habitual New Yorker's poetry has appeared in several anthologies, collections, and other amalgamations of words. His first full-length collection, *Ism is a Retrovirus*, was published by Three Rooms Press in 2011. Several chapbooks, including *clouds gradually undrape the moon* (2012), have been released by Neuronautic Press. He is a founder of the long-running Neurounautic Institute Poetry Workshop at the Auction House in New York City. Matthew would prefer to be a noun verbing than a gerund.

JOSEPH KECKLER is a singer, writer, and interdisciplinary performance artist. His most recent work, *I am an Opera*, was commissioned by Dixon Place, New York. Other performances have taken place at South by Southwest, New Museum of Contemporary Art, Merkin Hall, Joe's Pub, Performa, Issue Project Room, and BAM Fischer. The recipient of a Franklin Furnace Grant and a Fellowship in Interdisciplinary Work from New York Foundation for the Arts, Joseph has been awarded multiple residencies at MacDowell and Yadoo. He is currently working on a new EP and collection of essays.

DEAN KRITIKOS is a student first and foremost: of English at St. John's University, and of Poetry in the world at large. His creative work can be found in *NYSAI*, *Walk Write Up*, and *Crack the Spine*, while his critical work is forthcoming in *Oceanic New York* and *War Literature and the Arts*. When he's not reading or writing, he's teaching or tutoring—or, best of all, working construction.

ELIEL LUCERO is a native New Yorker, actor, bartender, poet, and DJ. His work appears in *International Poetry Review*, *Barber Shop Chronicles* (Penmanship Books), and in *gape-seed* (Uphook Press). Eliel has also produced and appeared in several "Sticky" plays (Blue Box Production), and been resident DJ for the LouderARTS Project.

CATFISH MCDARIS' most infamous chapbook is *Prying with Jack Micheline and Charles Bukowski*—one of over twenty-five publications. His work can be found in numerous national and international journals and has been translated into French, Polish, Swedish, Arabic, Bengali, Tagalog, and Esperanto. Twenty-five years of Catfish's published material is in the Special Archives Collection at Marquette University, Milwaukee, Wisconsin.

KEVIN MCLELLAN is the author of *Tributary* (Barrow Street, 2015), *Shoes on a Wire* (Split Oak, 2015), and the collaborative chapbook *Round Trip* (Seven Kitchens, 2010). He is the winner of the 2015 Third Coast Poetry Prize and his poems appear in journals including *American Letters & Commentary*, *Crazyhorse*, *Kenyon Review*, *Salt Hill*, *West Branch*, and *Witness*. Kevin lives in Cambridge, Massachusetts.

TATYANA MURADOV has been writing poetry for over ten years. She was born in Moscow, Russia, and raised in a small town in Texas. She moved to New York two years ago and has been a part of the poetry scene in the city performing for spoken word/slam teams such as LouderArts and Urbana.

NKOSI NKULULEKO, a nineteen-year-old poet and musician hailing from Harlem, New York, has performed his written work at places such as Apollo Theater, National Black Theater, Nuyorican Poets Café, Schomburg Center for Research in Black Culture, and the Senegalese-American Bilingual School. In addition, Nkosi has been recognized by the Scholastic Art & Writing Awards, is a nominated poet for the 2015 American Voices Award, and was a part of the 2014 Urban Word NYC Slam Team that went to the International Brave New Voices Festival.

EDGAR OLIVER is a playwright, performer, and poet in New York's downtown theatre community. Among his most important achievements are three acclaimed one-man shows: *East 10th Street: Self Portrait with Empty House* (Fringe First Award, 2009 Edinburgh Fringe Festival), *Helen & Edgar* (2012), and most recently, *In the Park*. The New York Times' Ben Brantley called Edgar "a living work of theatre all by himself," and described *Helen & Edgar*, (an extract of which is in this anthology), as "utterly absorbing."

BRI ONISHEA is a want-to-be gypsy, an ardent lover of words, and an amateur in many things who hopes to pursue a lifetime of art and learning.

MATT PASCA is the author of *A Thousand Doors* (JB Stillwater, 2011), and his poetry appears in numerous journals and anthologies. After earning degrees from Cornell and Stony Brook Universities, Matt signed on at Bay Shore High School where he has taught since 1997. He also advises the award-winning magazine *The Writers' Block*, acts as copyeditor and reviewer for the Long Island Authors Group, and teaches workshops at colleges, conferences, and continuing Ed. programs. His second book, *Raven Wire*, is slated for release in 2016.

LINETTE REEMAN is a nineteen-year-old queer poet from the Jersey Shore. Linette has represented Loser Slam at the National Poetry Slam, Individual World Poetry Slam, and Women of the World Poetry Slam. After becoming Rowan University's Grand Slam Champion, she represented them at the College Unions Poetry Slam Invitational. Linette is also a contributing writer to the online magazine *Bitchtopia* and enjoys watching videos of birds.

LYNETTE REINI-GRANDELL is the author of *Approaching the Gate* (Holy Cow! Press, 2014) and her poems have appeared in *Revolver*, *Poetry Motel*, and great weather for MEDIA's *It's Animal but Merciful* and *The Understanding between Foxes and Light*. A student of oral traditions, rune-lore, and circumpolar mythology, she lives in Minneapolis, strikes fear into the hearts of her students at the local community college, and performs regularly with the Bosso Poetry Company.

ELIZABETH ROSNER is a poet, essayist, and novelist. Her third novel, *Electric City*, was published by Counterpoint Press in 2014, alongside her newest poetry collection, *Gravity*, from Atelier26. Her first novel, the international award-winning *The Speed of Light*, was translated into nine languages and is currently in development as a feature film to be directed by actress Gillian Anderson. In addition, Elizabeth's second novel, *Blue Nude*, was named one of the *San Francisco Chronicle*'s favorite books of the year.

KARL ROULSTON cobbles together words, bellows them out, then honks on his wheezy blues harp. Find his work in the great weather for MEDIA anthologies *It's Animal but Merciful* and *The Understanding Between Foxes and Light*.

THADDEUS RUTKOWSKI is the author of the novels *Haywire*, *Tetched*, and *Roughhouse*. All three books were finalists for an Asian American Literary Award, and *Haywire* won the Members' Choice award given by the Asian American Writers Workshop. Thaddeus teaches at Medgar Evers College and the Writer's Voice of the West Side YMCA in New York. He is the recipient of a fiction fellowship from the New York Foundation for the Arts.

KEN SAFFRAN has had poems published in the *Amsterdam Quarterly*, *San Francisco Peace and Hope*, *Ambush*, and *gape-seed* (Uphook Press). He lives in San Francisco because he can't afford it.

FLOYD SALAS is an award-winning author of four novels, the memoir *Buffalo Nickel*, and two books of poetry. *Tattoo the Wicked Cross*, his first novel, earned a place on the San Francisco Chronicle's Western 100 List of Best 20th Century Fiction and also, along with *Buffalo Nickel*, is featured in *Masterpieces of Hispanic Literature* (HarperCollins, 1994). His manuscripts and papers are archived in the Floyd Salas collection in the Bancroft Library, University of California, Berkeley.

JON SANDS is the author of *The New Clean* (Write Bloody Publishing, 2011), and the forthcoming *The Love Hustle* (Rattapallax Press). His work has been featured in the *New York Times*, as well as anthologized in *2014 Best American Poetry*. He is the co-founder of Poets in Unexpected Places, a facilitator with the Dialogue Arts Project, and the Interviews Editor for *Union Station Magazine*. Jon is also a Youth Poetry Mentor with Urban Word-NYC, and teaches creative writing at both Bailey House (an HIV/AIDS service center in Harlem) and the Positive Health Project.

SARAH SARAI's poems may be found in numerous journal and anthologies including *Ascent*, *Yew*, *The Wallace Stevens Journal*, *Posit*, *Say It Loud—Poems about James Brown*, *The OR Panthology*, and *Lavender Review: Poems from the First Five Years*. Her online chapbook, *I Feel Good*, was published by Beard of Bees in 2013. Sarah's hobbies include mashed potatoes (thinking about and eating them), and politics.

BRIAN SHEFFIELD started seriously writing poetry in Monterey, where he attended California State University. With support from professors, friends, family, and some local bookshops, he released and distributed several chapbooks, got published in local zines and literary journals, hosted and facilitated poetry events, and taught creative writing and poetry to high school and college students. He recently moved to New York in order to experience a larger community of poets. Brian has been published in *Ishaan Literary Review*, *The Waggle*, *Hot Mess Zine*, and more.

REBECCA AUDRA SMITH is a feminist queer poet living in Manchester, England. She has an MA in creative writing from Manchester Metropolitan University, and has guested and been published by Loose Muse. Her performance piece "We Are All Equal Now" is featured on the online media project, *Imagining Equality*. Rebecca writes about sex, lesbian sex, and has a piece about bikini waxing forthcoming in the Bloodaxe anthology, *Raving Beauties*.

JOSH STEINBAUER is a filmmaker and poet. Probably his worst job ever was at a beef jerky plant in Minnesota—he came home from work one day and cried about it in the shower.

DEBORAH STEINBERG's writing has been published in *The Café Irreal*, *Necessary Fiction*, *The Red Line*, *Shelf Life*, *Monkeybicycle*, *Blood and Thunder*, and other journals. She is the fiction editor of the online journal *Rivet: The Journal of Writing That Risks,* and a founding editor of Red Bridge Press. Deborah lives in San Francisco where she facilitates writing workshops with a focus on healing, serves on the board of the literary reading series Bay Area Generations, and sings in the a cappella group Conspiracy of Venus.

PETER C. SWINBURNE is a New Zealand-American videographer-banjoist and the author of several drawers of fiction and screenplays. He lives in Washington, DC.

MATTILDA BERNSTEIN SYCAMORE is the author of a memoir, *The End of San Francisco* (City Lights Publishers, 2013), a 2014 Lambda Literary Award winner. She is also the author of two novels and the editor of five nonfiction anthologies, most recently *Why Are Faggots So Afraid of Faggots?: Flaming Challenges to Masculinity, Objectification, and the Desire to Conform* (AK Press, 2012), an American Library Association Stonewall Honor Book. Mattilda has just finished a third novel, *Sketchtasy*—an extract of which is included in this book. She lives in Seattle.

RACHEL THERRES is an artist teacher and a Baltimore girl in a New York world. She co-curates both Suffern Poetry and the Urbana Poetry Slam, competing in the National Poetry Slam in 2013 and 2014. She is decades in the thick of this world and still unraveling, baffled and awed. Rachel believes in poetry and community.

BRUCE WEBER is the author of five books of poems and several chapbooks, including *The Curious Adventures of Belinda and Mark* (Soncino Press) which also features the work of Bob Hart and Joanne Pagano Weber. Together with the guitarist and composer Nelson Alexander, they formed The No Chance Ensemble which regularly performed throughout the New York area from 1996 through 2012. By day, Bruce is the Curator of Paintings and Sculpture at the Museum of the City.

GINA WILLIAMS lives and creates in the Pacific Northwest. Over the years, she has worked as a firefighter, reporter, housekeeper, caregiver, veterinarian's assistant, tree planter, gas station attendant, technical writer, cocktail waitress, and berry picker. Her writing and visual art has been featured most recently by *Carve, Fugue, Palooka, Boiler Journal, Black Box Gallery, theNewerYork,* and *Gallery 360.* Gina's photography has also appeared on the covers of the great weather for MEDIA books *Debridement* by Corrina Bain, and *meant to wake up feeling* by Aimee Herman.

SARAH WOLBACH received her MFA (and a postgraduate fellowship) from the Texas Center for Writers at the University of Texas. Her poems have been published in journals including *Artful Dodge, Southwestern American Literature, Many Mountains Moving, Malpaís Review, Cimarron Review, Mudfish,* and *Paragraph.* She won second place in the 2015 Annual Writing Competition of the Women's National Book Association. Sarah lives in Santa Fe, New Mexico, where she volunteers at a wildlife rehabilitation center.

EMMA WOOTTON is a poet, dancer, and dreamer with a penchant for fancy journals. She is also unable to survive a day without coffee, and her poetry is often fuelled by caffeine and emotion simultaneously. Dipping in and out of the northern poetry scene that Manchester (England) has to offer, she is always out seeking new inspiration from the queer artists around her.

AMY WRIGHT is the Nonfiction Editor of Zone 3 Press, and the author of four poetry chapbooks. Her work appears in *Drunken Boat, Tupelo Quarterly, Quarterly West, Bellingham Review, Brevity, DIAGRAM, Western Humanities Review,* and *Denver Quarterly.* She was awarded a Peter Taylor Fellowship for the Kenyon Review Writers' Workshop. Amy lives in Tennessee.

JEFFREY CYPHERS WRIGHT is a New York City artist, eco-activist, publisher, impresario, critic, and poet. His thirteenth book, *Party Everywhere*, is out from Xanadu. In 2014 he directed a feature film, *The Key Ceremony*, about his experiences in East Village community gardens. Jeffrey currently produces the art and poetry showcase, *Live Mag!,* and is also the art editor for *Boog.*

great
weather
for MEDIA

Founded in January 2012, **great weather for MEDIA** focuses on the unpredictable, the bright, the dark, and the innovative. We are based in New York City and showcase both national and international writers.

Visit our website for information about our weekly reading series, events across the United States and beyond, submission calls, publications, and to sign up for our newsletter and blog.

Website: www.greatweatherformedia.com

Email: editors@greatweatherformedia.com

Twitter: @greatweatherfor

Facebook: www.facebook.com/great.weather

Instagram: www.instagram.com/greatweatherformedia

great weather for MEDIA titles

MORE

ANTHOLOGIES

Before Passing

I Let Go of the Stars in My Hand

The Understanding between Foxes and Light

It's Animal but Merciful

COLLECTIONS

Wil Gibson, *Harvest the Dirt* (Forthcoming, 2015)

Corrina Bain, *Debridement*

Aimee Herman, *meant to wake up feeling*

Puma Perl, *Retrograde*

Praise for our books

"These annual anthologies and other work by great weather for MEDIA are an admirable contribution to arts and culture." —*Ruth Latta, The Compulsive Reader*

"Corrina Bain writes poems as mean as the headlines, as true as a scalpel. Bain knows that what looks like savagery can be salvation, and has written us love poems from the church of the wound." —*Daphne Gottlieb*

"Visceral, insistent, beyond transgressive, *meant to wake up feeling* does just that."—*Anne Waldman*

"I haven't felt this way about a book of poems or a poet since the first time I read Charles Bukowski back in the 70's . . . *Retrograde* is one of the strongest, most surprising, and sublimely splendid collections of poetry I have ever read."—*Michael Dennis, Today's Book of Poetry*